Gypsy King – Julie Shaw

In the hour of your greatest success are sown the
seeds of your own destruction

(Gypsy proverb)

Matthew 13:39 – 42   And the enemy who planted
the bad seed is the devil.

Chapter 1

May 1971

Violet Lee sighed as she stepped out from the door of her trailer, sweat dripping from her forehead. Normally a slim woman, she could barely cope with all this extra weight when she had so much to do, cleaning, bleaching and polishing, to prepare for the new arrival. Being heavily pregnant didn't prevent a gypsy woman from keeping her caravan absolutely spotless, nothing did.

'What are yous fecking looking at?' she yelled at a group of the neighboring busy bodies, watching her with interest, 'go on with ya's, I've no heart for your gossiping today!'

The other women scurried away, on with their business, just as Violet knew they would. She had a fierce reputation on the site and she knew that men, women and chavvies often referred to her as Violent Lee because of her tendency to fight if the need arose. Even at nine months pregnant and ready to drop she wouldn't hesitate to clip any of them if she felt they deserved it.

Violet sat heavily on the wooden steps and swept her long black hair back from her hot face, a sudden gust of wind blowing up dust that stuck to her skin. Even though it was only May, the weather was as hot as any summer she could recall. Surely it must be today, she thought, as she felt another enormous jolt to her innards. This baby was fighting to be born, or at least it felt that way. Violet stroked her tummy, lovingly and whispered, 'I think you're going to be a boxer, my boy, I really do.' A wave of nausea swept over her and she leaned back on the steps to take a few deep breaths until the feeling subsided.

Her bump had dropped over a week ago and everyone knew that meant the birth was imminent. There'd be no doctors or midwifes for this baby, the generations of Roma from whom Violet descended had all given birth in their own homes with the only assistance coming from the elder women on the site, one of whom, in Violet's case would be Bina, the Drabadi, the old fortune teller and healer. Some of the younger women, and in particular, the Irish travelers, opted to go into a hospital these days, to give birth, but Violet didn't trust being anywhere she hadn't cleaned herself, and nor did she trust that the doctors and nurses washed their hands properly. Her baby boy would be born at home.

Home for Violet, and her husband Bo Lee, was a beautiful trailer on a council site at West Bowling in Bradford. As sites go it wasn't the biggest or the best by a long shot, but it suited Violet. This one consisted of just 16 caravans, a toilet and shower block for those who didn't possess them, and it was surrounded by woodlands. Only a ten minute walk to the main roads that led onto the townie areas, but one would never know this. Once tucked away on the site, it felt like you were miles away from civilization. Previously they had lived further south but on much bigger sites. But bigger sites, meant more people, and more people meant more aggravation in her opinion. Her husband being one of the instigators usually. Bo Lee also had a fierce reputation especially when he had the booze inside of him. A huge specimen he was too, six feet two and built like a brick shit house, he wasn't a man to be messed with. Like his father before him, Bo was striving to become known as a Gypsy King or King of the Gypsies, a self appointed title that no man would quibble if it had been earned by deed or justified declaration.

In the last two years, a lot of the Gypsies had taken offence to term Gypsy and were insisting on being called Roma or Romany, but Violet didn't care, she was proud to be what she was and had been called a lot worse over the years. At the age of 32 such things meant little to her, as long as she had her beautiful caravan with the luxurious soft furnishings and her beloved horse brasses and ornaments, she was happy. At least she would have been if she hadn't endured years of the other women whispering about the shenanigans of bloody Bo Lee!

As a provider, Violet couldn't fault her husband, he always saw her right and ensured she had the best of everything, but at the end of the day, he was a man. Since he'd been a boy, Bo Lee had always chased the gorger gels. The non Gypsy women who lived in the towns. He hated townies with a passion, especially the men, who he thought were weak as they didn't have their women under control, and led restrictive mundane lives. But he hated the women too if the truth be known. The sluts who wore disgusting clothes and made up their whore faces even in the middle of the day. Bo Lee was very vocal to the other men about how vile these specimens were and would often say that the gorger women's only purpose was to have their ugly heads smashed into a mattress while he emptied his sack into them.

Violet had always known how Bo felt and turned a blind eye to the flyers he had when the fancy took him. There was nothing she could do about it anyway, but when she had got pregnant, and Bina, the old hag who was the fortune teller had assured Violet that she was having a son, everything changed. Bo Lee swore he would never look at another woman again, that she was his one and only and that a son was all he had ever wanted, to carry on the Lee name. This had pleased Violet no end. She had begun to think she'd never fall pregnant in recent years, and had often secretly cried herself to sleep as she'd watched the other girls, one by one, giving their men the bouncing babies they craved. This little boy was going to be the most loved chavvy in the world, both Bo and Violet would see to it.

Her thoughts were broken when she heard her friend, Della Wright calling her name. She looked up and smiled at the blond woman making her way across the dirt. Della was lovely, one of the three Irish traveler families living on the site and with four young children of her own. Violet could never understand how such a large family could live comfortably in a small, two bedroomed caravan, but the Wrights seemed to take it all in their stride.

'I was away with the fairies for a minute there, Della,' Violet laughed, 'where are the chavvies? I love chattering with the little gel, Daisy, she's such a comic.'

"Oh, they're with their daddy,' Della said, squeezing herself onto the step beside Violet, 'mucking out the horses, so our little Daisy will be giving him hell right about now I should imagine, but, Vi, I had a vision this morning and I'm so excited! You're little one will be born today, I can promise you that. Clear as day it was.'

Violet smiled, 'oh I hope you're right, Della, this heat is killing me off and I'm just sick of being so heavy now.' She leaned and arched backwards on the steps trying to move the gnawing pain that was settling in her lower back.

Della reached out a hand to feel Violet's swollen stomach and looked worried as she continued.

'I'm always right, Vi, you know that, and by looking at you I don't think we'll have that long to wait. In fact, I think you ought to get yourself into the bed, Vi, I mean it. I'll go get the others if you like, so we can all be ready.'

Violet knew that Della was speaking the truth, she did seem to know these things, and having had four children of her own it was no wonder. If she was being honest with herself, she did feel a bit funny, hot sweats now accompanying the aches, so she heaved herself up off the steps and held onto the rail to steady herself. As she did, she felt the unmistakable gush of what she knew were the waters.

"Holy hell, Della,' She said, 'you're right, it's coming and now. Leave me be and go round the women up. I'll get to the bed. Don't forget to bring Bina, we will need a blessing when this is all over.'

Della ran off while Violet hobbled inside and into the cordoned off area that served as the marital bed. Despite the worsening pains, she grinned a huge grin as she hoiked up her long skirt and lay herself down. As soon as this baby was born, Bo Lee had promised her a brand new trailer, with all the modern trappings, including two, real bedrooms. That thought made the current pains more bearable.

'Come on, baby boy,' she whispered as she stroked her swollen stomach, 'your mammy can't wait to meet you.'

As she lay, the pains growing more agonizing by the moment, Violet allowed her mind to wander elsewhere. She did this often, when things got too much for her, and it usually suited her to recollect every piece of her precious Capo Di Monte. Her beloved ornaments, each lovingly chosen by her Bo Lee, and each costing an absolute fortune!

All the other women envied her, she knew that, and her van would be filled with the most jealous ones, every Monday when she took the ornaments from their display cabinet to carefully dust them. She sometimes took out her collection of Crown Derby too, just to cement the fact that she had it all. And very soon, in the next few hours anyway, she really would have it all.

Today however, she chose to think about Bina, the seer, and her assurance, long ago, that her Bo would soon have the son he longed for. His one desire – a healthy son to carry on the Lee name. That had been before. Before the tragedy that had trampled on all of their dreams. Violet winced and drew her legs up, knowing this would soon be over, but still, she forced herself to remember. She had kept this particular terror at bay for two years, but she knew now that after she played it out this one time in her mind, she would finally be healed. She barely noticed the women filing into her bedroom, nor their voices urging her to push.

She was back in the summer of 1969, heavily pregnant with her blessed boy, and hanging out the washing. She had been smiling as she heard the whistles and shouts from the lads in the field behind her, as they tried to break in a particularly cantankerous wild filly. So taken was she in hanging out the bright new terry toweling nappies she had just bought and hand washed, that she didn't hear when the shouting turned louder and more desperate. In fact, she only found out what had happened when she woke up in hospital, broken bones, a terrible headache and a dead baby boy.

'Push!' Screamed Della, 'come on, Vi, he's almost here!'

Broken from her painful memories, Violet screamed out as she gave one final push. Before she passed out, she smiled as she thought of her husband's happiness.

Chapter 2

Maureen King was in a jovial mood. She'd already sank a few Gin and tonics in her favourite boozer, The Brown Cow, and she was out with some of her mates from the Canterbury estate, one of whom was now trying to entice her up to dance.

'Aw come on, Mo,' Sue Gorman pleaded, 'It's the Elgins, I thought you liked Motown, get up!'

Maureen giggled and finally pulled herself unsteadily to her feet, 'go on then,' she laughed, as she teetered on her new high heels, 'let's show these blokes at the bar what they are missing out on.'

'You're a bloody married old battle axe now, Mo,' Sue chastised, 'you just leave them blokes alone, and besides, you'll know about it if Big Pat comes home unexpected and cops you flirting!'

The Brown Cow was only a small pub without a real dance floor and not many places to sit down either. The locals joked that the carpet was that sticky with spilt beer that once you got somewhere to stand in there, you were rooted. It wasn't exactly easy to dance upon, but Maureen was determined to do her best. And she would flirt too if she wanted. It had been a while since she'd been out after having the two babies in quick succession, so when a neighbour's kid had called round asking for a babysitting job, Maureen hadn't needed asking twice.

'Big Pat's working away till Monday,' she yelled across to her mate, before winking outrageously at one of the men at the bar, 'so, while the cat's away and all that.'

'Behave, Maureen!' Sue said as she tried to turn her friend towards her, 'you do know that they're all gypsies? Stop gawping for God's sake!'

Maureen didn't care a jot. She knew she had a reputation as a bit of a girl where the men were concerned, and she'd dated a few Gypsy blokes in her time. In fact before she married Pat she had been putting it about anywhere and everywhere. Those wild days were what Maureen considered to be the best days of her life and she often resented getting married and settling down.

Her husband, Big Pat as he was known, was a great provider. As a local criminal he had his hands in a lot of pies and had brought himself up through the ranks. He could never understand why his wife never wanted the big house in the countryside, the jewelry and the expensive trappings that they could afford these days, but Maureen was a council estate girl through and through and wanted her kids to be brought up as she had been.

'Oh my God, Sue!' She said suddenly, gripping her mate's shoulder, 'don't make it obvious, but is that Bo Lee standing over by the juke box?' Maureen used her friend for cover as she tried to hide herself from sight. It had been a good few years since she'd seen that face, and it wasn't one she had wanted to see again really, not after they'd almost got caught out by his wife.

Sue tried to make it appear as if she was being casual as she did a little spin, 'I think it is,' she said, facing Maureen again, 'why? You know him?'

'I did do, a lifetime ago,' Maureen said, suddenly not in the mood for dancing, 'come on, my feet are getting glued to this fucking carpet, let's sit down.'

Sue squashed onto the bench seat next to Maureen and picked up her drink, 'well I've heard he's a right evil bastard, doesn't he do some work with your Pat?'

Maureen nodded before draining her own glass, 'now and again their paths cross as far as I know,' she said, 'but I don't trust them Pikeys, I've told Big Pat he should find some other fucker to deal with.'

Sue laughed then, 'Oh, Mo, you're a right one, you are. It's not that many years ago when you used to have your tongue hanging out for anything with a dodgy accent. What's good for the goose is good for the gander, I'm sure Pat knows what he's doing, mate.'

Maureen laughed too then, mainly at her friend's cheek and bravado for calling her out. Not many would do that and live to tell the tale, but she'd known Sue for years. The woman wasn't wrong though, there was just something about those men that got her going. It wasn't really the accent, or the coal black eyes that did it, but the way they didn't give a shit about anything or anyone, and didn't even pretend to be gentle when they were after a bit of the other. Or, she mused, it could just be the smell of them, a mixture of the countryside and sweat. Whatever it was, looking at Bo Lee still got her all hot and bothered and it was making her slightly uncomfortable. Being married to Big Pat gave her everything she wanted so the last thing she needed was temptation in her path.

'Shut up, Sue,' she said in a mock hurt tone, 'how is it my fault that the gyppos happen to be exceptionally good in the sack? And anyway, I'm a happily married woman these days. Come on, sup up and let's fuck off down to the Bull while I've still got soles on my shoes.'

The two giggling women staggered out onto Little Horton Lane and linked arms as they sang their way down the road to the Black Bull.

***

Bo Lee took a drink from his pint and stared through the mirror behind the bar. That silly cow, Maureen King and her mate had been making a show of themselves. Pissed as farts and trying to get male attention, just like all the gorgers always did. Thank God they were leaving and hadn't recognized him, things at home were good right now and the last thing he needed was to be tempted into fucking things up. No, distractions like that were a thing of the past, at least for now. He'd made promises to his wife and intended to keep them this time. He would make those same promises to his baby son when he was born too.

"hey, Bo,' Bent Stanley said, nudging Bo in the side, 'wasn't that Big Pat's woman? The one with the all the legs and the fancy heels that's just left?'

Bo turned slowly and pretended to look. He shrugged and took another swig from his glass, 'I don't know, I never saw her face,' he lied, 'but it wouldn't surprise me. I hear Pat is away for a few days, and if his woman is like the rest of them, she'll be making the most of his absence.'

Bent Stanley had earned his nickname due to an unfortunate accident during horse and cart racing that had left him partly crippled and unable to walk upright. He had refused hospital treatment, despite his broken bones, and it had taken months of being laid up in his trailer before he could even stand. Although Bo trusted the man, he liked to keep his private business with non Gypsy men like Big Pat King, away from men off the site. The less others knew, the less chance he had of getting caught doing illegal deals that didn't concern them. It was mainly shifting stolen good to other parts of the country, and providing cars to be used in robberies, but a lot of the other gypsy men didn't like getting involved with gorgers, no matter what the reward.

He slapped his friend on the back, 'anyway, fuck the women, let's have some more ale, it's your round.'

Stanley laughed and turned back to their other friends at the bar, 'How comes it's always my round?' He joked, 'hang on, don't tell me, it's because I'm as bent as a copper's wife and I deserve it?'

Bo Lee laughed along with him, 'got it in one, my friend,' he said, passing his empty glass, 'a pint of the swill these fuckers have the cheek to call bitter, and keep it cold whilst I go for a piss.'

He was just giving it a shake, when bent Stanley almost fell through the toilet doors,

'Bo, come on, quick. It's your missus!'

Bo zipped up his pants, his Violet would never venture into a pub, so there was no hurry, 'course it is, Stan,' he laughed, 'like she'd ever step foot in this fucking dump.'

'No,' Stanley said, 'I mean, she needs you, Bo, one o' them ugly fucker twins has been in, Bill Callaghan's kid, Violet's having the young 'un, she's in labour.'

Bo Lee waited while Bent Stanley climbed into the passenger seat, then set off at full speed in his Transit van back up to the camp, grinning like a dog with two tails. Today was definitely a good day.

Chapter 3

1985

Mirela Lee was stunning. At just 14 years old she was already the subject of much attention from most of the older boys on the site. With her mother's long, black hair, and her father's curls that hung down her back, she couldn't walk anywhere on the site without the boys ogling her. Today was no exception. She was pushing a huge navy and silver pram around, trying to hush the latest baby for his tired mother, when she heard the wolf whistle. She spun her head around to see who it was this time.

'You get yourself on, Jimmy Jackson,' she called out in a mock chastising tone, 'or my daddy will beat the sweet Jesus out of you.'

Jimmy Jackson was 18 and had been laying tarmac with his dad all morning, so was covered in dirt and the black stuff. He winked, but the threat of Bo Lee was always enough to stop things going any further. Everyone knew that Bo was fiercely protective of his daughter, and everyone knew why.

Until the minute she'd been born, Mirela was meant to be a boy. It had been forseen by Bina, but she'd been very, very wrong. According to site whispers, Bo Lee had been distraught that his child had not been a son, and he and his wife, Violet had never had another one.

'I can look if I don't touch,' he called back cheekily, causing Mirela to blush and turn away.

She giggled as she stopped to fuss the baby while Jimmy walked across the site to where the other men were. Mirela quite liked the attention from the boys and she knew she looked good today. It was the middle of summer and they were having a long spell of glorious weather which meant that she was allowed to wear her hot pants and T-shirt around the site. The tight top also meant that she could show off her recently acquired breasts to their full advantage.

Already a tall girl, Mirela was used to hearing the women tell her what a beauty she was, and how she was blossoming into a fine young woman. And now she was of age, just like all the other girls, she was encouraged to slacken off a little on the modesty and was allowed to flaunt her body in order to attract a possible mate. Except that for her, attracting a mate had never been an option.

The only blight on her life was the fact that her daddy had always insisted that she must marry a Lee boy. A cousin, which would most likely be Chrissy Lee, the bully of the bunch, but the only one left who hadn't already chosen his woman. Mirela hated Chrissy with a passion, and he was the reason that she'd argued with her mammy yet again only this morning. Mirela had eventually stormed out of the caravan to calm down, but her mammy's words lingered in her head, 'you know what you caused me, girl, you'll do as your father says. It was written the day you were born, and there's nothing either one of us can do about that.'

'A penny for them?' It was Della Wright, her mammy's friend, come to peep into the pram, 'oh, what a little sweetie he is,' she cooed as she tickled the baby's chin. 'Makes me get all broody so it does.'

'It's mammy, as usual,' Mirela said, sighing miserably. 'We were so close before, when I was little, but now, it's like she hates me or something. She just can't see that Chrissy Lee is no good for me, and I don't want to marry him. I won't marry him. I heard her arguing with daddy ages ago, trying to get him to change his mind, so she must hate the boy as well, but she won't bend. And, Della, I'm only a bloody child myself!'

Della ran her hand, lovingly through Mirela's curls, 'oh, sweetheart, your mammy doesn't hate you, she loves you. Unconditionally. It's just our way, sweet pea, you know that. You need to carry on the family name, that's all it is.'

Mirela got angry then, why could no one see why she didn't want this? 'But no, Della,' she said, 'It's not unconditionally, not at all, it's all about the bloody family name! That's all I hear about. Why? Just because I wasn't a boy and they never had a boy, that's not my fault is it? Why should I have to pay the sacrifice for that?' She glared at her, daring her to dispute the facts, because she couldn't. Everyone knew the truth, but they never took her side, they simply tried to justify her parent's actions and it wasn't fair.

Della shook her head, 'girl, the Lee name goes back for generations, and your father is far too proud for it to end with him. I know, I know, there are cousins who are boys who will ensure the name goes on, but your daddy wants your children to be Lees too. That's all it is. And you know, they say it's better the devil you know for a reason, girl, if it hadn't been Chrissy Lee, it would have been someone else your daddy picked.'

'But it's not fair! Why should either mammy or daddy have a say?' Mirella shouted, tears springing to her eyes. This was never how she imagined her future would be. She had been happy to leave primary school at the age of 11, to not go on to the big school like all her friends had, and to take on the role of cook, cleaner and baby minder for any of the other women, but at least she thought she'd get to marry the boy of her dreams and have lots of children by him.

Someone who made her heart flutter like what happened to the girls in the books and magazines that she had read, someone perhaps like Jimmy Jackson, who was big, strong and funny, not to mention good looking. Certainly not a cousin like Chrissy who had a big nose and a mean spirit.

'Life isn't always fair, my little chickadee,' Della soothed, 'but spare a thought for your mammy, she also had her life mapped out for her without having a say in it herself, and she and your daddy are happy enough. They have all they could ever want and more, and that's what they want for you, my sweet, that's all it is.'

Happy enough? Mirela thought, is that the best she could hope for then? And even if it was, who the hell would want to settle for the happy enough that her parents had. They were always yelling at each other, and that's when they could be bothered to communicate at all. Her mammy said that she and dad were like ships that passed in the night these days. Oh, he took Mirela off with him for a trip out now and again, and they'd have a laugh together, but back in the trailer, when they were all together, the silence was usually deafening.

'Yes well,' she told Della, defiance punctuating her words, 'times have changed, and I'm of a different generation. I will not be bound by my daddy's stupid ways. The laws of the bloody traveler!'

'Please, child,' Della implored, sadly, 'try be happy with your lot and don't fight the inevitable. The sooner you accept how things are for women like us, the better you will feel. My Daisy is only a couple of years older than you, sweetheart, and very soon, we'll be choosing a husband for her too, just like my daddy did for me. We're not like the city folk, Mirela, going through all the heartbreak of one boyfriend after another, all that stress is taken out of our hands, and we should be thankful for that.'

'Daisy is almost 17, Della! Yous haven't forced her into a marriage yet. How come she gets to grow up first?'

'I'm not saying these things should be rushed, chickadee, but when the time is right, Daisy will marry too, and we will be approving her suitor, but she's not ready yet, Daisy was a late starter, not like you, Mirela, please try to understand it's for the best. It was always going to be different for you. The boy you would marry was picked for you years ago, we've never had anyone in mind for our Daisy.'

Mirela stared at the woman she'd known all her life, a beautiful woman herself, and wondered how she could so easily fall into line. Della could have had anyone and anything she wanted, yet all she ever wanted was to produce babies, cook and clean. Did none of these people want more from life? Mirela had read many books and she knew for a fact that life didn't have to be this way, it was exciting and thrilling, and falling in love was what happened. Girls could take from life whatever they wanted, they could get real jobs and work for a living, just like the men did. They didn't need someone else giving the orders and bringing home the money, forcing them to stay home.

'Well, I won't accept that, Della,' Mirela said, suddenly feeling very sorry for herself, 'I won't be like you and my mammy, and I shall tell daddy exactly that when I go out on the road with him later today.'

She then leaned into the pram to tuck the blanket around the baby, so the sun's hot rays didn't burn the little fellow, before turning away from Della and walking towards the trees where it was shady. She glanced back to see her mammy's friend shaking her head sadly before heading off herself.

****

'I don't care how many times she says it, Della,' Violet raged, 'I can't do a fecking thing about it, can I? Yes, I hate that she's betrothed and has been since the day she was fecking born, but it's our way!'

'His way, you mean,' Della said in barely a whisper, hating to upset her best friend, but feeling it was necessary. 'Yes, he needed to find her a husband, but did it have to be that monstrosity?'

'No, Della! Don't you dare start all that shite again, don't you dare. You with more kiddies than the old woman in the shoe, holed up in that dingy van all fecking day, cleaning and mopping up sick while he's on the road, drinking and whoring, just don't fecking start that with me.'

'Violet, I'm not for starting with you, I'm not. It's just your Mirela, well she wants more than we had, and who can blame her? She's of a different generation, all the young ones are wanting more, and mine'll be the same. They will, and we can't pretend any different. My Daisy would have a heart attack if I told her she must marry now, and especially if it was a boy she hated!'

Violet opened up her beautiful van door and held it, 'go on now, Della, please, before I say something we'll both regret. If you were any other woman living here, I'd have put your lights out for getting in our business, but you're my friend and let's keep it that way.'

Della looked like she might say something else but thought better of it. Couldn't risk one of Violet's legendary smacks. Instead, she simply shrugged and made her way past the angry woman and walked down the steps.

'I'm sorry, Vi,' she said, 'I won't upset you again, I promise, and you're right, it's not my business. You're a good friend and I know that like me, you only want the best for your girl.'

Violet was shaking as she closed the door behind her friend. She put on her polished brass kettle, took out a china cup and saucer from the cupboard, and through her tears she made herself a cup of tea. No one knew what she'd gone through over the years, trying to fight for her daughter to be seen as worthy by her own father. For the longest time Bo had hardly acknowledged he had a child. It had been a bitter pill to swallow, everyone knowing her husband had simply given up on her just because she had given birth to a girl and not a boy, and it was only after Mirela had developed her own cheeky personality at around the age of five, that Bo had taken any interest in the poor child whatsoever.

Because Mirela could swear like the lads as a little tot, and was happier living in jeans and trainers than in the fancy dresses worn by all of the other little Roma girls, and because she would fight with anyone who dared cross her, Bo finally accepted her as his own.
He would show her off at trade fairs, declaring she was as fit and strong as any of the lads, he took her scrapping and tarmacking in the early days and taught her everything she needed to know about horses. It was too little too late as far as Violet was concerned though. She had sank into a pit of depression, locked in her own anguish.

Unfortunately, this had meant that Mirela was left to her own devices, neglected by her mother, often relying on the other women on the site to wash and feed her, and getting a reputation of being something of a wild child, which suited Bo down to the ground, it was almost like having a son. It had taken years before she had been able to pull herself together and be a proper mother to her child.

When Bo started making sexual demands of Violet, in her bitterness, she rejected him. 'You take that rancid, filthy meat away from me,' she'd yelled, accusing him of laying with the gorger women, 'out there, spreading your fecking seed among the muck, then fetching it back to feed me your sloppy seconds, well I don't want it!' That day, something had changed in their already fractured relationship. It was as if a door had finally closed and would never again be re-opened.

Violet sat down with her tea, gazed around her beautiful van and sobbed. She and Bo hadn't slept together since Mirela was five years old, but there was no getting out of this sexless marriage. Bo would never leave her, it wasn't their way.

And even if he did, Violet could never take another man – not that she would want one, because their tradition meant that if she did that, the shame brought upon her would mean that even her daughter would be shunned, and no man would have her. Mirela thought she had it bad, well the little madam would have many more harsh lessons to learn in this life, and she best get used to it.

Chapter 4

Patti King's mother had just informed him that she was getting ready for the pub and that he'd have to keep an eye on his younger sister. This wasn't anything new, his mother practically lived in one boozer or another whilst his dad was working away, and watching his sister, Danielle, was a regular occurrence. Not that he had plans or anything, but it irked him that she just assumed he had nothing better to do.

'For fuck's sake, mother!' He yelled from his bedroom, 'I'm not your personal, built in babysitter! Why can't our Danni go out with her own mates? I do have a life you know.'

'Stop that language, you little shitbag!' Maureen yelled back, 'and you'll do as you're told, lad. I've told you, I'm out for the day, and I don't want your sister stuck indoors all bloody summer. If you're going out, you'll take her with you, do you hear me?'

'It's okay, Patti,' Danielle whispered as she passed the bathroom and peeped in, 'just tell her you will, and you don't have to really. I'll find someone else to knock about with. Beverley Hostie said I can go round to hers any time I like and listen to her new tapes.'

Patti stopped combing his hair and turned to grin at his sister, 'nah, sis, we can go together and find some trouble to get into. I'm just winding the old woman up. Go get dressed, I won't be long.'

Patti King was 16 and had left school just before the summer holidays, his sister Danielle, at 15 still had another year to go. The expectation had been that Patti would either get a job or start working for his dad, Big Pat, but neither options suited Patti just yet. He and his sister got by just fine. Despite him moaning at his mum, he actually enjoyed it when she pissed off to the pubs and left them to their own devices, and he really didn't mind spending time with Danielle. Both liked skipping school and hitting the town to do a spot of shoplifting now and again, and both enjoyed the odd bottle of cider in the woods when the weather was nice. Their dad was hardly ever home, always taking care of business, which Patti now knew meant something illegal, and their mum, well if she wasn't partying at one of the local boozers, she was either sleeping it off or getting ready for her next jaunt, as she was today. The kids could get as pissed as they liked most of the time without anyone ever knowing about it.

'Go on, piss off downstairs or go get dressed while I finish getting ready,' Patti said, pushing his sister out the bathroom and closing the door. 'I'll think of something to do.'

Danielle giggled and ran off to her own room. 'I'm getting dressed, mum!' She shouted downstairs, 'our Patti said I can go with him.'

***

Maureen King smiled to herself as she added another layer of ruby red lipstick. She felt lucky she had such good kids who did as they were told. Some of her mates had right mardy little fuckers who they were bringing up. All mouth and no manners, but she'd brought her two up right. No thanks to Big Pat of course, who was rarely at home for more than a few days, but that didn't bother her. Bringing up two children practically single handed was a small price to pay considering the rewards. A man feared by everybody but herself, who was happy to allow her to do her own thing, and still dropped her a wad of money every time he came home. What more could a woman want?

'A few less bleeding wrinkles, that's what!' Maureen said to the mirror as her thoughts made her take a closer look at herself. Her lipstick had already started bleeding into the fine lines around her lips, and the more powder she pressed onto the dark circles under her eyes, the more her wrinkles appeared to deepen.

'Oh, bollocks to it!' She said, as she gave her reflection a sultry smile, 'I look better than most for my bloody age, and I still have the men fawning after me.' She smoothed down the yellow, off the shoulder, tight fitting dress she was wearing and slipped her feet into her strappy, matching sandals. Giving her glossy brown hair one final bump up with her fingers, she checked her gold watch and knew that her taxi would be waiting on the street for her.

'Right, kids, I'm off!' She called from the hallway, 'behave yourselves and I've left a few quid on the coffee table. Make sure you get something from the Wimpy or chippy with it, don't be blowing it in on bleeding cider, you kids think I'm frigging stupid!'

Closing the front door on her way out, she slyly glanced at next doors twitching curtains. *Go on, nosey Susan, take a bleeding look!* Maureen thought as she plastered on her biggest smile and made a big thing out of getting into the taxi. *Jealous, the frigging lot of 'em.*

***

His mother safely out of the way, Patti grabbed the ten Rothman's and card of matches he had stashed under his mattress and sauntered out onto the landing. 'You ready, sis?' He called towards Danielle's room, 'I've got some fags if you wanna share one in the back garden.'

Danielle didn't need asking twice. She flew out of her room, fastening the button on her flared jeans, before tucking the black T-shirt into the waistband. 'Coming! Patti does this top look alright? Mum hasn't washed my checked shirt.'

Patti grinned. Most of the other 15 year old girls he knew, wore skimpy skirts or shorts in this weather, but his little sister was a bit of a tomboy and preferred jeans and T-shirts. This didn't bother him though, as it meant that the lads on the estate tended to leave Danielle alone which was a good thing. At fifteen, it was a rarity to find an untouched female around these parts, and the last thing Patti wanted was to have to fight some twat in order to defend his sister's honour.

'You look fine, kiddo,' he said as they went out into their neat back garden, 'do us a glass of Pepsi and I'll save you two's on this ciggie.'

'What we gonna do today, Patti?' Danielle asked as she waited for her half of the cigarette, 'it's boiling hot so I don't fancy going round the shops, can't we go to the park or something. I could roll my jeans up and we could have a paddle in the pond.'

'A paddle in that fucking death trap?' Patti laughed, 'you'll catch all bleeding sorts. No, I'm after earning a bit of dosh this summer but I need to check something out first. I've got an idea. Bit of a walk, but if it all works out I'll be sorted.'

'Shall we call to Nannie Dot and grandad Patrick's on our way?' Danielle asked, 'they'll most likely give us a bit more money, what d'ya think?'

'I think, no.' Patti said, it's alright for you, but nannie Dot can't stand me, and it does my head in being nice to her, the old witch.'

Dot and Patrick were in their 70's and were Big Pat's parents. They lived in a council house on the same estate and it was immaculate, but Dot's mouth was as dirty as a dockers and she never held back whenever Patti was around. It was like she hated all the male species apart from her son. The last time Patti had been forced to call there, it was to drop his granddad some money off from his dad. It was a given that the old man would take it straight round to the bookies to have a gamble with, but nanny Dot had of course blamed Patti, screaming at him that he was just like every other man, determined to torment the poor women who spent their lives taking care of them.

'She might throw money at you, sister dearest,' Patti concluded as he locked the back door, 'but as far as I'm concerned, she's tighter than a nun's chuff, now come on.'

'You make me laugh, Patti, tighter than a nun's chuff! You know, with the things you say, you're more like Nanny Dot than you'd like to think.'

Half an hour later, it was a good job that Danielle had opted for long jeans as she scrambled after her brother on all fours through trees and bushes to give them the vantage point they needed for Patti's big idea. 'This is your big plan?' She hissed, 'Mick Keenan's bloody scrap yard? Jesus Christ, Patti, great bleeding idea this is!'

'Hush!' Patti whispered, 'his dogs might be prowling, I'm just making sure that noncey Graham isn't still helping out here. I heard he got run out of town, and if it's right, I'm gonna try get his job.'

Graham Garland had worked for Mick Keenan for years but he'd recently been arrested and dragged away from the scrapyard in hand cuffs after a schoolgirl had reported that he'd given her chocolate and then forced her to let him put his hand in her knickers. A group of locals had been praying he got out on bail before sentencing, and he did. That was the worst thing that could have happened for Graham, as within hours of being back on the streets, he disappeared into thin air. The rumour mill said that he'd been ran out of town, whilst those in the know seemed to think that he was hiding within some six foot concrete foundations that would soon be helping to hold up a new block of flats on Manchester Road. Whatever had become of Graham Garland, there was absolutely no one worrying about the warrant for his arrest that had been issued.

Chapter 5

Mirela was nervous. Bo King had, as usual, shouted across the site for her to join him on the drive out to Mick Keenan's scrap yard. It was something they enjoyed doing together, and Mirela knew that by pretending she didn't mind getting dirty and helping unload a pick up van load of scrap metal, she made her dad happy. She wasn't the son he had always yearned for, but she always tried her best to make up for it. She often went so far as removing any girlie clothes, such as summer dresses or clingy tops before her father was due home and would replace them with scruffy jeans and a baggy T-shirt. Today however, she figured that for what she had to say, she may as well also upset him by showing more flesh than usual.

'You alright then, my little mush?' Bo asked as they drove over the bumpy, muck road that led them off the site. 'Only you got a dodgy look on you, girl, your Ma been mithering you again?'

Mirela stole a glance at her dad. A huge, handsome man, with hands like shovels. The size of him was enough to make any man fear upsetting him, but Mirela had no such fear, not usually anyway. He was obviously in a very good mood and she knew he was teasing her. He hadn't said a word about being dressed like a young hussy or anything. Maybe now that she was a teenager he expected her to be a bit more girlie.

'I'm fine, dad,' she answered, quickly turning to face the road. Suddenly her nerves were kicking in and she began to think that perhaps today wasn't the day to have it all out with her dad after all. Her intentions had been to tell him she'd made her mind up and it was final. She would not entertain the idea of marrying Chrissy Lee or even having anything to do with him at all, and, in fact, she'd marry a man of her own choosing. Thank you very much! Instead, she resigned herself to shelving the idea for another day. After all, Della had informed her that the ugly Chrissie Lee would be off again very soon, visiting relatives in Ireland and helping them break in some new horses. That might take months so at least she had a bit of time to work on her dad. Maybe the gods would even shine on her and Chrissy Lee would meet the woman of his dreams, fall in love, marry her and stay in bloody Ireland. Changing the subject, Mirela glanced back and nodded towards the empty pick -up part of the truck.

'No scrap for Mick today, dad? Are we buying something from him?'

'I got a few big jobs lined up for the lads,' Bo said, 'and I've a feeling our Mr Keenan can help me get my hands on a few cement mixers that I'm going to be needing.' He glanced towards Mirela and added, 'it's gadje talk though, little mush, so I'll need you to sit with the truck while me and him have a chin wag.'

Mirela nodded, she was used to her dad having his private chats with people, and she knew it wasn't her business. Gypsy children were brought up to understand literally that children should be seen and not heard. It didn't bother her in the slightest to be left to her own devices. 'I'll sit by the truck, dad,' she said, 'I like to be in the sunshine.'

Having arrived at the scrap yard, Mirella watched as her dad strode across the rocky dirt path to where Mr Keenan's portacabin was, then, looking around, she saw a relatively smooth, grassy area where she decided she'd sit and sunbathe for a while. But not to dwell on her fate, she decided, it was too nice a day to depress herself further. It was times like this that she wished she had accepted that Sony Walkman her dad had offered her a few months earlier. She loved music but had never been into gadgets that much and she thought all the kids looked a bit weird carrying their songs around with them.

***

Ten feet away from Mirela, behind the perimeter bushes, Patti King and his sister were watching the olive skinned girl with interest. She appeared to be making daisy chains as she plucked the tiny white and yellow flowers from the ground and carefully looped them together.

'I'd give *her* one!' Patti whispered as he turned to grin at his sister, who immediately punched him in the arm.

'You're disgusting!' Danielle whispered back as she scrambled further into the hedge to get a closer look, 'oh! I know who that is, she used to go to my school.'

'You do?' Patti asked, feeling an opportunity coming on, 'well let's go have a chat with her then, old friends and that, come on, you can introduce me.'

Danielle grabbed hold of Patti's top and prevented him from moving, 'stop it, you divvy! It was ages ago. My junior school, St Michael's, she probably doesn't even remember me. It's Mirela Lee, gypsy Bo's daughter. Patti, we can't just go through there, it's embarrassing!'

'Well, you'll never know if you don't ask,' Patti said as he grabbed his sister and pushed her headfirst through the bushes before scrambling through after her.

'Oh, hiya!,' Dannielle spluttered to a startled looking Mirela, as she tumbled out from the bushes, red faced, 'I'm so sorry, we didn't mean to scare you.'

Mirela stared at Danielle and then beyond her as Patti was next through, a big grin on his face.

'You alright?' Patti said as he patted his hair back into place, 'I haven't seen you up here before, you know my sister don't you?'

Danielle saw that Mirela didn't appear to recognize her, so she took the lead, 'You're Mirela Lee aren't you? It's me, Danni, Danielle King, we were in the same class at St Michael's. We used to play horses every day in the playground.'

'Oh yes, I remember you now,' Mirela said, smiling shyly, stealing a glance at Patti, 'and you too, you're her brother. You were the year above us.'

Patti gave a dramatic bow, 'Patti King, at your service,' he said, grinning, 'and I must say, for someone so pretty, I can't believe I don't remember you.' He winked then and went on, 'but ten out of ten for remembering me, I must have made an impression eh?'

Mirela blushed an even deeper shade and dipped her head slightly before turning to look nervously in the direction of Mick Keenan's cabin. If her daddy could see her just now, he'd have kittens.

'Oh, don't be worrying about the fellas,' Patti said, 'if it's business, they could be ages, and knowing Mick, they probably will be.'

Danielle decided to try impress the girl, 'my brother might be working up here soon, for Mick I mean, he's friends with our dad too, so you might be seeing our Patti around quite a bit if you come here all the time.'

Patti watched with increasing interest as the beautiful girl seemed to take in what his sister had said, processed it and then wondered what to do with it. He laughed and play punched Danielle, 'don't be scaring the poor girl off already, Dan, for all she knows we might be right wrong 'uns. We're actually very nice people,' he went on, 'quite angelic if you want the truth.'

Mirela laughed then too, 'it's nice to see you both again, I don't get out much. Off the site I mean. When I left primary school I never got to go to secondary. I chose to stay on site and look after the women and the babies and stuff, so it makes a change to bump into different people.'

'Oh my god!' Danielle exclaimed, 'so you never had to go back to school, that's mental. I wish I had that bloody choice! Jesus, I'd give anything not to have to go back to that shit hole.'

'Oh, it's not as fun as it sounds,' Mirela said, 'I often miss the company of my old friends, and it gets boring doing the same things day in, day out. But, it's the Roma way, and I have to do what's expected I suppose.'

'Well then,' Patti said, 'that settles it. It's summer, come out with us and have some fun. Tell your mam and dad you've met up with some old mates, and get out for a few hours, it'll be ace.'

Mirela's face darkened a little as she answered, 'I'm not allowed. My kind can't just go off, unchaperoned, especially with non gypsy girls, and definitely not with boys. It's not fair really, but it's the way we live.'

Just as Patti was about to impart some words of wisdom, he noticed Bo Lee stepping out from Mick's cabin. He ducked down and grabbed his sister to follow suit as he edged back out of sight, 'leave it with me,' he whispered to a nervous looking Mirela, 'don't worry, I won't get you in trouble, but I'll think of something.'

'So, who were the gorgers that you were talking to?' Bo asked, as they reversed out of the scrapyard. 'What were they doing up here?'

Mirela almost had a heart attack. She was sure her daddy hadn't seen them. 'I'm not sure about the boy,' she answered, cautiously, noticing her daddy was watching her with a funny expression on his face, 'but I think the girl used to go to my old school, I'm sure I recognized her.'

'And what were they doing up this neck of the woods, eh? Probably casing the place, and they say that we gypsies are all tramps and thieves.'

Thinking fast, Mirela decided to play safe, 'I don't know, daddy,' she said, 'they just appeared a minute ago and asked me my name. I felt bad for the girl in case she remembered me, but I told them to piss off.'

'Good gel,' Bo said, laughing heartily, 'country trash, the lot of 'em. You give 'em it both barrels, my chavvy, if they bother you again. Especially that gadje, he looks a queer 'un does that.'

Mirela laughed too and agreed. But even as she did, she just knew that somehow, someday soon, she would definitely be seeing Patti King again. She also knew by the fluttering of her heart that she certainly hoped he would bother her again. She leaned forward to turn on her Daddy's radio to avoid any further conversation, and knew instantly it was sign, as her favourite song came on halfway through - *there must be an angel, playing with my heart.*

Chapter 6

Danielle was teasing her brother later when their mother burst into the kitchen, where they were joking around.

'What did you just say? A fucking what?' She demanded, 'you're going out with a fucking pikey? I bleeding well hope not, son,' she spluttered, holding herself steady on the door frame, 'or your dad'll have a bastard fit!'

Danielle dropped her head, sorry that she'd landed her brother in the shit. Her mother was mean when she was drunk. She'd been out at the pub since opening time and two minutes ago she'd been snoring away on the sofa, but she needn't have worried, Patti wasn't going to give in that easily.

'Oh, he will, will he?' He asked, 'and what would he say if he knew you'd been out on the pop all day, leaving us to fend for ourselves again? He'd be thrilled about that I bet. As usual you've come in halfway through a conversation and got the wrong end of the stick like you always do. We were just saying how we met a gypsy lass when we were up at Keenan's yard, so get your facts right.'

Maureen tried to strike out at her son, but she staggered into the kitchen cupboard instead, banging her hip into the side, 'cheeky little mare,' she said, wincing as she rubbed her hurting hip, 'you'll get a good hiding if you don't watch your trap, and what were you doing up at Keenan's anyhow? It's your sister's bleeding school holidays, lad, not yours. You're meant to be out looking for a job, because mark my words if you don't land one before your father gets back, you'll be working for him, make no mistake.'

Maureen had obviously forgotten her train of thought as she staggered back into the living room, 'lazy little fucker!' She yelled before slamming the door.

'Don't worry about her, Danielle,' Patti said, grinning at his sister, 'she'll have forgotten all about us by the time she's slept it off. You seen the state of her? She's a mess.'

Danielle shrugged, she loved her mum who always looked out for the pair of them – in her own way, but she hated it when she was drunk and it was usually her brother who copped for it if she was in a bad mood. 'I don't like her shouting at you like that, Patti,' she said, 'and I don't want you working for our dad. He has to deal with bad men all the time, Patti, he told me that himself, they get into fights and all kinds of trouble, please don't get involved.'

'You think I'm that daft, sis?' Patti laughed, 'you think I want to go out collecting his debts and shit, worrying about getting my head kicked in every time I step outside? No fear, Dan, stop stressing. Mick Keenan pays good money, I'm going to work for him, you wait and see.'

'Oh, and it's because he pays good money is it?' Danielle asked, giggling, 'nothing to do with the fact that a certain gypsy girl goes up there now and again. I can read you like a bloody book, Patti King.'

'Who?' Patti asked, feigning innocence, 'the apple doesn't fall far from the tree, sis, you're as mental as our mother.'

*****

In spite of what he had said to his sister, Patti lay in bed that night, unable to sleep as thoughts of the beautiful Mirela ran through his head. He had never been in love before and wondered now if this is what it felt like. He tried to think of anyone he knew to take example from, but he couldn't.

His grandparents certainly didn't come across as a couple who had ever been anything other than at war with each other. His granddad only ever smiled when he was being handed money from either his dad or his nan. He'd smile then, a big fat smile as he grabbed his coat and set off to the bookies.

His nan, well he didn't ever remember her actually smiling. Only ranting and raving about what shit bags men were, and how kids these days had no discipline and were all short of a few slaps. Patti grinned to himself as a childhood memory crept into his thoughts, his nan had fallen asleep on the sofa one afternoon when he and Danni had been round there. She was snoring loudly and they were laughing at her. Danni dared Patti to pluck out this long hair that was sprouting from their nan's chin, and he did. He got such a slap, but it had been worth the laugh. No wonder the old bat couldn't stand him.

Then there were his parents, were they in love? Well, his dad always slobbered over his mam when he'd been away working and came back home, his mam always cooked him his favourite meals, and dad was always buying her presents, but that couldn't be love, Patti figured, because they hardly spent any time together. Despite all the gifts and the shows of affection, his mam couldn't wait for his dad to be back off to work. She took his money then asked how long he'd be home for. No, that wasn't how Patti felt about Mirela. If he could snag a girl like that, he'd never leave her side.

After a fitful night's sleep, Patti was awake at dawn. He usually had to be dragged from his bed around lunchtime, but he had some serious thinking to do, and as he tossed and turned the night before, the morning couldn't come soon enough. He crept downstairs avoiding any creaking floorboards. He and his sister had got used to that years ago, often sneaking out late at night to go party with mates, they knew every dodgy stair and loose board in the house. After a quick breakfast of cornflakes and orange juice, Patti quietly unlocked the front door and left the house. He felt a little guilty about not waking his sister to go with him, but he figured that Danielle would only get bored by what he was hoping to do. Bored or scared shitless. Either way, best he kept her out of it for now.

Not sure quite what he planned on doing, Patti sat on the front doorstep for a few minutes to think. He sparked up a cigarette and inhaled deeply as he turned to look back on the house. No one would be up for ages yet, so he had some time. He tried to sort his thoughts out. First and foremost, he intended on seeing Mirela somehow.

Second, he had a long walk across to West Bowling to where the traveler site was. He checked his pockets for money just in case he'd need any, four and a half quid, that would do. It wasn't like he could take the girl out on a date or anything at this time of the morning. Third and final thing, before he set off, he patted his jeans pockets and grinned as he felt the foil wrapped package. His mam would go ballistic when she realized he had nicked off with her best roast beef. Patti wasn't stupid, he knew that every gypsy site would be well guarded by hard bastard dogs.

It took him a good half an hour to get there, but he hadn't walked fast, more like a slow stroll as he went over and over what he should say if he should get caught, and more importantly, what he should say if he actually saw Mirella. For all he knew, she might not have given him a second thought after she and her dad had left Keenan's. She might think he was a right plonker just turning up where she lived, uninvited at that. He began to have second thoughts.

Don't be a pussy, lad, he told himself as he finally got to the end of the dirt road leading to the site, *turn on that Patti charm and she'll be eating out of your hands.* Charm, that's what his careers advisor had said he had bucket loads of, on the last day of school. Patti had been surprised the bloke even knew him, he'd spent that much time bunking off, and when the time came, most of the teachers couldn't wait to see the back of him.

'Not one O'Level and just 3 CSEs,' Mr Malpass had stated, shaking his head, 'god knows where you'll end up, Master King, in one of her Majesty's big houses, no doubt. However, if you put that charm of yours to good use, you just might end up with a job. God help us all.'

Patti grinned as he recalled the school and the teachers he'd never see again. Who needed a job when everything was already out there for the taking? Some of the blokes who worked for his dad couldn't write their own names, let alone take an English exam, and they were earning absolute fortunes. Concentrating on the task at hand, and hearing the dogs barking as he approached the site entrance, he retrieved the beef from his pocket.

'Here, boy!' He hissed as he tore a piece of meat and threw it towards one of the three German Shepherds chained to a post. Seeing the dog gobble the treat down, he started to throw more and inched closer to them. Patti loved dogs and they could always sense it, it wasn't long before he was standing with them, ruffling their necks and feeding them beef from his hands. 'There we go, mutts,' he said softly as he searched beyond them for any signs of life. He was careful to stay low however, the vans and trailers were mere yards away and he didn't want to get caught. It was one thing to charm the dogs but quite another to explain himself to a dozen or so angry Gypsies.

Satisfied that he had the dogs onside, Patti moved back a few feet so he could settle himself behind a couple of trees and still keep watch without being seen. He'd always known about this site, but never actually seen it close up. To his estimation there were around 20 or so trailers scattered around in a rough semi – circle shape.

Not at all uniform, some set back nearer to the big trees that lined the site, whilst others were more central, nearer to what appeared to be a communal area – definitely a place where children played given the amount of bikes and scooters that were lying around there. Patti approved, always hating the confines of his family's council house, he imagined it would be like being on holiday every day, living somewhere like this. It seemed that people were starting to wake up on the site and one or two were emerging from their caravans. A woman in her 40's was the first to walk out, holding the hand of a little girl who looked to be around three years old.

 'I never pissed the bed, nannie!' The young girl was shouting, 'please don't tell my auntie Nee, I think it was granddad who done it.'

'You come over there with me now,' the woman shouted back, 'and tell your auntie what a dirty little chavvy you are! Blaming your fecking granddad indeed!'

Patti giggled as he watched the scene, and then he saw a couple of the men walking to what looked like a shower block or something. They were carrying towels, so he assumed that's what it was. Pretty soon, the site had sprung to life. Kids running around, half naked in the early sunshine, yelling and laughing as they played, women chatting to each other from their van steps and a couple of older lads were lighting a fire in some kind of pit. Still no sign of Mirela though, or her dad for that matter.

It had been over an hour now and Patti's legs were starting to get cramp. He badly needed to stand up and stretch but if he did that he risked being seen, or getting the dogs excited again so he tried to get comfortable by sitting rather than squatting as he had been. His patience paid off eventually, and after another hour he finally saw her. She must have stepped out of a van without him noticing, and she was now pushing a battered pram around, and giggling at the baby inside. It took Patti's breath away as he watched, his heart beat speeding up at an alarming rate, but Mirela really was just beautiful. Her long hair, loose and wavy, bounced on her shoulders as she pushed her way across the uneven gravel and dirt. Patti blushed as his eyes wandered to her breasts to see if they too bounced.

Please make her come this way, Patti pleaded silently as he got back into his squat position, *come on, Mirela, turn around and come this way.* Finally, she did just that, and as she wandered closer to the gateway near Patti, he could hear her voice as she chatted to the baby.

'Oh, you're such a. little beauty,' she laughed as she bent into the pram, 'just look at those chubby little cheeks, oh you'll break a few hearts, baby boy, for sure.'

Not sure what to do to get her attention, Patti decided to stand up and show himself. 'Mirela!' he hissed, 'it's me, come talk to me for a bit.'

Mirela spun around and looked terrified when she saw Patti, but after frantically checking behind her, she rushed towards him.

'Oh, my sweet Jesus!' She said, 'are you crazy, Patti King? My dad'll have your guts for garters if he finds you up here, move back into the trees or something, what on earth are you doing?'

Patti grinned and edged back into the trees, urging Mirela to follow him.

'Told you I'd come find you, didn't I?' He grinned, 'man of my word, me. Don't worry, I haven't been spotted by anybody.'

Patti saw the range of emotions cross Mirela's face as she struggled for something to say, she looked both afraid and excited, something that pleased him immensely.

'Look, I know you can't come off with me or anything,' he said, 'but I just had to see you, Mirela, I couldn't think about anything else, and if this is all we can do, then that's okay by me.'

Mirela's face lit up and she smiled and touched Patti's arm, sending waves of electricity through his body.

'I'm touched, Patti,' she said softly, 'really I am, and I wish things were different, but I tell you what, my dad is taking some scrap engines up to Mr Keenan's tomorrow, I could ask if I could go if you like. Will you be there in the morning?'

Patti smiled, such unfamiliar feelings stirring through him, 'Course I'll be there,' he said, 'I'll be there first thing and I'll wait for you.'

Mirela looked back at the site, 'okay, well I'll see you there then,' she said, 'I have to get back now with the baby, his mammy will be looking for me, but I promise I'll see you tomorrow.'

'What about a kiss to keep me going till then,' Patti asked cheekily, moving towards her. He was still shocked however when Mirela leaned forwards and softly kissed him on the lips.

'Just one thing, Patti,' she said as she started walking away, 'you must bring Danni with you too. If it's just you I won't be allowed to talk with you, but if she's there with you, dad won't stop me.'

Still stunned by the soft, warm feel of her lips, Patti nodded like an idiot. He'd have agreed to bring his mam and his nan too at that point if it meant seeing her again. He ran all the way home without realizing how he even got there, so jubilant he was at the morning's events. Nothing could top this, he thought, nothing.

Chapter 7

Patti was besotted and he wasn't about to let
anyone spoil things. Big Pat, his dad had arrived
home unexpectedly the night before and had told
Patti that he would be expecting him to put a few
hours graft in this week, but Patti had no intention
whatsoever of that happening. So, at 7.00am the
next day, he was in his sister's bedroom, shaking
her awake.

'Come on, Dan,' he whispered, 'it's time to get up.
Don't forget you promised to come with me.'

'Oh, piss off, Patti,' Danielle grumbled as she tried
to turn away and fall back to sleep, 'and besides,
dad said you have to go to work today.'

'Fuck dad!' Patti hissed, 'I'm seeing Mirela and
that's that, and you promised you'd come with
me.'

Danielle sat up and rubbed the sleep out of hers,
'Patti, it's only bloody seven o'clock, what is wrong
with you?'

'Just get up, Dan,' he said, 'she said she'll be there early, and I want to be well gone before dad gets up, come on.'

Danielle dragged herself out of bed, 'piss off then, while I get dressed,' she said, 'though why I have to go too, is beyond me. I won't be doing this every day, Patti, I mean it.'

Patti grinned and left her to it. His sister wouldn't let him down and he knew she understood why she had to come. He'd explained it all the night before, and though the concept was alien to both of them, they knew it was the done thing in Gypsy culture. A young girl absolutely could not be alone with a boy, in fact she couldn't be anywhere off the site, unaccompanied, and that was that. And although Patti felt a bit of an idiot, his sister trawling along with them, that's exactly what had to happen in order to see Mirela.

In fact, it happened almost every day that week. Big Pat seemed to have more on his mind than finding gainful employment for his son, so at least temporarily it was quite easy to get out and find Mirela, and that's exactly what they did. A couple of times at the scrap yard, and then three times at the Gypsy site. Each time, Patti warning his sister to give them a bit of space so they could talk privately, and each time, Danielle getting more pissed off with her brother.

'She was actually *my* friend, Patti,' she said on one occasion, as they approached the scrap yard, 'and you've just muscled right in there and the pair of you leave me out. Why should I get up early just to act like a mug for you? It's the summer holidays you know, I'm missing out on spending time with everyone else!'

'Please, Danni,' Patti begged, 'I swear as soon as I can convince her to sneak off with me, I will do, and then you can stop coming with us.'

'Oh, nice one!' She said, 'so you'll just dump me when it suits you then, eh? What am I meant to do with myself then, Patti? All my mates are pissed off with me for never doing anything with them, but you don't give a shit!'

'Please, Dan!,' Patti begged, 'don't start, not today, mate, she's walking up here now, just hang back a bit, I swear it won't be for much longer.'

Danielle skulked back into some nearby bushes, fuming with her brother, and acted like she couldn't hear their pathetic simpering to each other.

'Is your sister mad with me?' Mirela asked, smiling into Patti's eyes, causing him to melt. 'I feel so bad for her having to trail around every day just so we can be together.'

'Nah, she's fine,' Patti lied, 'she knows how much we mean to each other.'

After a long kiss and some desperate groping, Patti had to pull himself away, 'Mirela,' he panted, his voice husky, 'I love doing this, and honestly, our Danielle will be fine, but me and you, well we need some proper time alone, don't you think?'

Mirella glanced back towards Mick Keenan's trailer. They were well hidden from her dad, but he'd only popped up to collect some money he was owed, and was already suspicious about Mirela begging him to take her along with him so often, so they didn't have much time.

'I've been thinking about nothing else,' she whispered, 'and there might be a way, Patti. My mammy never knows where I am most of the time, and if she looks for me, she assumes I'm out with dad or in someone else's van looking after the babies. I know for a fact that next Tuesday my dad's off to Appleby to sort out a piece of land he's buying, and he won't be back till late at night, I'm sure I could sneak off for a couple of hours then without being caught out.'

'Oh my god, that would be ace!' Patti cried, 'let's do it, Mirela. Where's Appleby?'

Mirela laughed, 'it's really famous!' She said, 'where the Gypsy and traveler horse fair is held, it's miles away, Cumbria, but I was there with dad in June and he put an offer in for a bit of land or something, so…'

'So, me and you have a date then!' Patti announced, grinning. 'Where and what time shall I meet you?'

Mirela flinched as she saw her dad emerging from the van down the field, 'Tuesday, ten o'clock, I'll be waiting on the muck road before the site.' She leaned in for one more quick kiss and then called, 'bye, Danielle, and thanks for all this. Bye, Patti.' And then she was gone.

'Oh, I love you, Mirela,' Danielle mocked as her brother joined her, 'I love you too, Patti, mwah! Mwah!'

'Shut up, you div!' Patti said, blushing as he play punched his sister, 'seriously though, Dan, do you think she meant this is it till Tuesday?'

Danielle stared incredulously, 'are you mental, Patti? It's only frigging three days away for god's sake!'

Patti felt stupid, but was still a bit miffed. What was he meant to do all weekend? His dad was still home too, so that wasn't good.

'The twat'll have me working for him, just you wait and see,' he acknowledged as they walked back home. 'I can see my dad fucking everything up, Dan, like always.'

'Well, if you'd have done what you said, and got a job with Mick, he wouldn't be able to would he?'

Just as Patti expected, his dad was on his back the minute they walked back into the house, only it was with very unexpected and very welcome news.

'You think you're still a kid, eh?' Big Pat raged, 'you think you'll spend the summer shop lifting in the town and loitering about the estate with the rest of these goons do you, lad?'

'No, dad,' Patti stammered, 'I have been looking for work, I swear, in fact I…' he was just about to lie and tell his dad Mick Keenan had work for him, when Big Pat grabbed him by the shoulders,

'Don't you dare utter a fucking lie to me, my boy, I'm warning you. Now your mother has told me what a lazy little fucker you've been since leaving school, and that stops now, do you hear me?'

Patti nodded, visions of going out debt collecting with his dad's gang of ugly mutts, and he desperately searched for something to say that would get him out of it, but his dad wasn't letting up yet.

'So, and this isn't up for negotiation, lad, I've got you a job myself. You're not ready to join the firm just yet, but I have a finger in a few pies, and you, my boy, will not let me down, you hear?'

Patti nodded, both relieved that he wasn't to join his dad's crew, yet worried about what was coming next, 'course I won't dad, I swear. What's the job?'

'What a fucking touch!' Patti laughed in the back garden as he shared a cig with his sister, 'I couldn't believe what I was hearing when he said I'd be doing four days a week up at the scrap yard. Remind me to give Keenan a pat on the back, sis.'

Danielle shook her head, 'if you fell in a bucket of shit, you'd come out smelling of roses, Patti,' she said, 'but tell me, how will you see your beloved Mirela now, eh? Stuck up there four days a week.'

'In case you're in any doubt, sister, there are seven days in a week, leaving me three to be elsewhere, and not forgetting Mirela goes up there with her dad all the time. Life just couldn't get any better.'

Chapter 8

Mirela cried outside her caravan. Her parents were raging at each other and as usual, it was all about her. She squished her hands up to her ears, but she could still hear the shouting and balling. It was the same argument she'd heard for years, only this time it was worse as it was getting closer and closer to the time she'd be forced to marry Chrissy Lee. What she couldn't understand though was why her mammy fought hard against it behind her back, yet to her face she told her she'd have to accept it.

'For God's sake, Bo, it's only her 15th birthday we're talking about,' her mammy yelled, 'she's still a fecking child!'

'She's no child, and she's no different to any of the other gels on here,' Bo yelled back at Violet, ' it's our way, you know it is! You're lucky I'm not dragging her to Appleby with me and Chrissy today, she needs to be spending time with him, before he sets his sight on some other gel. He's knocking on is the lad, he won't hang around waiting till madam decides she's ready. Use your common sense, woman!'

Mirela could hear banging and slamming from inside the van and she guessed that would be her mammy trying to contain her anger. Taking it out on the cupboards rather than do as some of the women did, throw the china around.

'She'll fecking hate you!' Violet yelled, 'and who can blame her, not me! As god is my witness, if you make her marry that fecking thug, you'll never have a days' peace for the rest of your life, Bo Lee!'

'Is that a curse is it?' Bo yelled back, 'because trust me, you've cursed me for eternity, woman.'

The trailer door slammed, and Bo stormed out and down the steps. He didn't notice his daughter as she sat, sobbing on the dirt.

None of what she'd heard surprised Mirela, it had always been so. She always knew her dad had wanted a son and was distraught to get a daughter, she always knew she was expected to marry a Lee boy, and she always knew there would be a big party thrown for her 15th birthday, coming up in just over a fortnight. As far as the Roma had always been concerned, you were a woman by that age, and had to do what was expected of you, no exceptions. What upset her most was what she perceived as her own weakness. Her complete inability to just speak her mind and fight for what she wanted. Her mammy had no problem speaking the truth if she felt it important, and her dad certainly wasn't bothered what anyone thought of him, so what made Mirela so timid when it came to fighting for her own happiness? She didn't know the answer of course, she only knew that she had to do something to stop the inevitable, or her life wouldn't be worth living.

'Baby girl, come inside,' Violet called from the top of the steps, 'your dad's gone off to Appleby, there'll be no more shouting, I promise you, come on in.'

'What's the point, mammy?' Mirela asked, 'just to hear you tell me how you tried your best, but that in the end, it has to be dad's way? Or maybe you'll tell me that I can actually be a normal teenager and that I get to go out and meet a boy of my own choosing, or even go meet up for a burger and a milkshake with some friends, hmm, is that it?'

Violet looked as beaten as her husband always made her feel, but Mirela watched the range of emotions flitter across her mammy's face.

'Mirela, I'm sorry,' she said, 'I don't know what else to do, but I promise you it's not for the want of trying, and I'll keep trying until I can do no more. But when all is said and done, you might just have to marry Chrissy and make the best of it.' Violet ventured down the steps and reached out her arms, 'please don't make things worse, my baby girl, life isn't so bad, even when you're stuck with someone not of your own choosing. The men, they go off and do their own thing, we woman can choose to have a good life, it's just all about making it work.'

'It's all about being submissive and doing as we're told, you mean, mammy, well I'm sorry but I'll fight it longer and stronger than you. I will not be married off, so if I'm to be thrown a party, do not expect me to play the expectant little virgin to that monster of a cousin!'

'You watch your mouth, young lady!' Violet yelled, 'and go on, get yourself off to another van for a bit because I'm sick to the back teeth of it, do you hear me?'

'Loud and clear, mammy!' Mirela shouted back, 'and don't worry, I won't be bothering you, I promised to do some cleaning today to earn some money, so I'll be out of your way.'

As Mirela walked away and in the direction of crazy Hilda's van, she heard her mother slam her trailer door. Not exactly how she had planned to sneak off to meet Patti, but it had provided her with the perfect opportunity. Her mother would be too angry to go asking around after her, and would assume she was off cleaning at Hilda's. The bat crazy, elderly Roma whom all the other kids were terrified of. Hilda would scream out foreign sounding chants at the top of her lungs, and threaten to curse anyone who would try to quell her. She didn't fool Mirela though, Mirela knew that deep down, Hilda had a heart of gold, and that she loved every child deeply, having never been able to have one herself. Today however, it was someone else she loved that she was going to meet.

As she made her way through the site, careful to be seen by certain people, and not seen by others, Mirela felt like she was seeing things for the very first time. Women setting out their stools and pots outside their vans. Later they would sit out there, peeling vegetables whilst chatting to friends about their men or their babies. Other women, carrying two or three babies across to the block to get them washed and clean, only to then watch them go rolling around in the dirt all day.

Some were already taking down their nets so they could polish their already gleaming windows. And the men? Well, they were no doubt polishing off a full cooked breakfast before heading out with their pals for the day to do their dodgy dealings. Yes, they'd earn from it, but the women wouldn't see much of it at all. They'd be given nice, shiny ornaments, food and the minimum amount of clothing they needed, but if they dare to moan about it, they'd get a slap.

Mirela knew her mammy was actually one of the lucky ones. Even though she and her dad barely spoke these days, he had never knocked her about, and had always made sure she had the very best of everything, he even made sure she had access to cash if she needed it, leaving her instructions on where he hid his money.

Not all of it, Mirela guessed, but certainly enough so that her mammy could go to the shops if she needed, without having to wait for her man to come home. It was what made the other women jealous of her mam, that and the fact they had to contend with violent men who liked to keep them in their place. However lucky her mammy was, Mirela just knew that she didn't want this life, and she wasn't going to accept it. Her determination made her quicken her pace as she started to jog the last of the way down the muck road to where she knew her Patti would be waiting for her.

'Oh, Patti, I've had such a horrible morning,' she said as he swept her into his arms, 'you'll not believe what they're all planning for me, not in a million years.'

Patti laughed, 'calm down and give us a kiss,' he said, 'I feel like I've waited a million years to see you!'

Mirela accepted the lingering kiss hungrily, but then tugged at his arm, 'come on,' she said, 'let's get away from this bloody place before some spiteful rat spots us and reports me or something. Honestly, Patti, I feel like an escaped bloody convict.

'Wow! Someone's really upset you, haven't they, bloody this and bloody that, well, my good news may cheer you up. Not only am I now site security at Mr Keenan's scrap yard, but I also have my very own trailer there at the bottom of the field.'

'You are kidding me?' Mirela said, her eyes widening. This meant something. She wasn't quite sure what, but she felt in her bones that things were about to change, 'what, like a proper trailer, to live in, by yourself?'

'When I say trailer, I don't exactly mean what *you* would think of as a trailer,' he said, grinning at her stupefied expression, 'it's more of a knackered old, damp caravan, with a rotting interior. And I don't live there exactly, I'll just stay overnight in it now and again, when Mick has business during the night. But, and this is what's important, it's hooked up to some generator, so I have power in there, a kettle and some cups and that, but hey, it's a start, and it's somewhere to hide out when we get time together.'

'My god, that's great!' Mirela said, 'somewhere to call our own. Oh, Patti, I'm so excited, but what about Mr Keenan? If you're meant to be working, how can we be in there?'

'Don't worry about him,' Patti said, 'he's a lazy fat fucker, he hardly ever ventures out of his cabin, and anyway, I've purposely been working my arse off for him over the weekend and making sure he knows it, so that when you come up, he won't mind me taking a few well earned breaks.'

Mirela soon realized that Patti had oversold his own trailer, even with his bleak description of it. As she stepped inside, the smell of damp hit her nostrils straight away, but also the unmistakable stink of wet dog. She took in the broken cupboard doors, the dirty upholstery and the threadbare curtains that hung from a rusty wire and tried not to breathe in too deeply.

'But, don't worry,' she said, after composing herself, 'It's nothing that a hammer, a few nails and a good clean won't fix. I'm used to getting my hands dirty, I'll soon have this place fit to sit in.'

'I hoped you'd say that,' Patti said, a grin spreading across his face as he reached into a rotting cupboard and pulled out a tin bucket filled with cloths and cleaning products, 'nicked this little lot from my mum's,' he said, 'not that she'll notice, our cupboards are filled to bursting with the stuff.'

So, while Patti sat on the bench seating, Mirela set to scrubbing windows, walls, doors, in fact every surface got the bleach treatment, 'and this is before I start,' she said, 'got to get rid of the bad stuff and then I can really clean.'

As she cleaned, she told Patti all about the upcoming birthday celebrations and how these Gypsy events were such a big thing, and that she couldn't get out of it. She almost stopped as she watched his eyes darken when she mentioned how Chrissy Lee would be there. She had poured her heart out a few days earlier about her predicament, and told Patti how arranged marriages were part of their culture. She hadn't realized how angry he would feel about it, so had played it down ever since.

'Don't worry, Patti,' she said, 'I'm going to make it very clear before then, that he's a cousin only, and that's how he'll stay.'

'It's all a bit fucking perverted if you ask me,' Patti snapped, 'and a bit noncey. He best not put his fucking paws on you, I mean it. He's not the only one who's got back up, you know, I could have him killed with just a mention to my dad or his lads. I know you say it's how things are up there, babes, but it's fucking wrong. Just get them all told.'

It pained Mirela that Patti was getting upset, but it also thrilled her to see the jealousy in him. As much as he could never understand the gypsy way of life, it was clear he truly did love her.

Chapter 9

Maureen King took a deep breath as she stared at herself in the dressing table mirror. All hell was breaking loose downstairs and she knew she'd have to go down and intervene or something, but she was livid. Those fucking kids of hers, causing shit as usual between her and Pat, and no one giving a toss about how it affected her. Big Pat was still at home, three weeks now, and he never stayed that long, but because frigging Patti had started working for Keenan, and frigging Danielle was saying she wasn't going back to school, her husband had decided he needed to be home more. Well, she wasn't having her life put on hold while he played dad of the year, not a chance. She leaned into the mirror and had one final poke about with her crow's feet, checked out how she'd look if she had her jowls lifted, then went downstairs.

'What the bleeding hell is going on?' She yelled as she burst into the living room, 'the fucking neighbours will be phoning the cops on us!'

'These two, that's what's going on,' Pat shouted, 'thinking they get to call the shots and flout the rules, that's what. Well, I make the rules in this house, and you, woman, have been letting things slide. I can see it now, they have no respect for either of us, and that's down to you.'

'Oh, piss off, Pat, don't you dare blame me. I do my best with them and they're a lot better than most of the kids around here, that I can tell you. To be honest it's your fault, pal, they're not used to having you lumbering around the pissing house for weeks on end, none of us are. You get moody because you're bored and it affects all of us.'

'Why won't either of you ever listen to us?' Danielle cried, 'It's nothing to do with dad being home, mam, it's just that he doesn't care what we want. I've been offered a job, a good job, running a stall in John Street Market, but *he's* saying I have to go back to school!'

'A *good job!*' Pat screamed, 'tell fucking Maggie Thatcher that selling knickers in the market is a good job, you stupid girl.'

'Stop it, Pat!' Maureen shouted, suddenly seeing her immediate future getting all messed up. She needed him to see she had control so he'd piss off back to work. Before she spoke next, she gave her daughter a wink. A wink that she knew Danielle would understand, 'okay, listen, Danni. Your dad's right, love, we want you to pass all your exams so you can get the best job you can, so you have to go back to school in September, however, I will go with you to the market, and we can sort out a Saturday job there for you, just for a bit of spends and to get you into working. How's that sound? You could offer to do all the school holidays as well if you like.'

Danielle, still breathing heavily, wiped her eyes and looked at her mum, 'well I suppose that would be a start,' she said, before then glaring at her brother who had remained silent, 'it will give me something to do at least!'

'And what's *he* supposed to have done?' Maureen asked, pointing at Patti, 'because I know he's taken the job you got him, and he's been getting up to go every day.'

'Yes, he's been getting up,' Pat yelled, 'but getting up what is the question! Mick thought it was a great joke telling me that my son has some tart that he takes up there, locking themselves in a shitty trailer. Well, he can sow his wild oats, he's old enough, but he does it in his own time, not on the clock, do you understand, lad?'

Maureen almost felt sorry for Patti as she watched him struggle between lashing out at his dad, or keeping the peace.

'Fair enough,' he said, 'but she's no tart, dad, we love each other.'

Pat seemed to soften a little at that and he sat down in his armchair, 'plenty of time for love, mate,' he said, 'and plenty of fish in the sea. If she's your first, you'll soon learn how painful love can be. Harden up, Patti, because if the devil should cast his net, it would be filled with women!'

'Charming!' Maureen said, thankful that at least for now she'd managed to restore peace. 'Now, Pat, talking about work, Sinead Hanley has invited us to her 40th next week, but I told her I'd let her know. I mean, it's fine, I can tell her no, I won't be going if you're away.'

'Go,' Pat said, 'enjoy yourself, Maureen, you deserve it, but if you're asking will I be here, then no, I won't. I've got a demolition job lined up in Derby, a big one, so it could be a couple of months.'

Her face dropped, 'that's a long time, Pat,' she said, 'what about wages for me?'

Pat laughed, 'not, oh, I'll miss you, Pat, just, how will you get my money, eh? Don't worry, my little love, one of the lads will be back every Friday and he'll drop it off for you. His wife actually likes him home for the weekends.' He stood back up, 'right then, that's me away to the pub for a couple of hours. I need to round another team of demo lads up, and as sure as eggs are eggs, that's where I'll find them.'

Maureen, though a bit miffed that Pat had gone off to the pub without her, was happy to know she'd soon be let off the leash, and could see nothing but sunny afternoons in a pub garden ahead.

'Cheer up then you two,' she said to the kids, 'no use having faces like slapped arses, your dad'll be off in the morning and no doubt he'll leave me a tidy sum to treat you both with.'

'Mum,' Danielle said, 'did you really mean about only Saturdays, because you know I'd split my wages with you, every week.'

Maureen thought about it and then came to her usual conclusion – anything for an easy life, 'fuck it, take the bleeding job, but if the board man comes around and catches you, I knew nothing about it, alright?'

Danielle grinned, 'thanks, mum, and course, I'll say I was bunking off if I'm caught, but I won't be. Oh, and take no notice of our Patti's maungy face, it's cos his girlfriend is being thrown a big party tonight, and he can't go.'

'Shut your face, Danni!' Patti growled, 'I don't need a reminder thank you very much.'

'Who?' Maureen asked, 'you still at it with that gypo lass? Fucking hell, Patti, you need to cut ties with that lot, I'm warning you. It'll only bring trouble to our door, lad, and anyway, why aren't you good enough to go to their fucking party?'

Patti stood up to go to his room, 'oh, mum, just leave it will you. I'll go out with who I want, and it's not that I'm not good enough, it's because they don't know about me. Keep her like a fucking prisoner up there they do, it's shit!'

Chapter 10

Mirela took a deep breath as she stared at the stranger in the mirror. She didn't recognize herself at all. Gone were the jeans and T-shirt, replaced by a grey and white checked, pleated skirt that only just grazed the tops of her knees, topped with a fancy, almost see through white blouse. She allowed herself to smile as she twirled for her mother.

'Here,' her mum said, handing her a pair of dainty, black court shoes, 'put these on, they just finish it all off.'

'Jesus, mammy! The party is outside, on the muck, I'll end up crippling myself in those.' Still, she slipped them on and had to admit she looked good. One of the twins, Mary Jane, had been over and styled her glossy hair and sorted out her make-up, Mirela just wished that her Patti could see her like this.

'Oh, you look beautiful, Mirela,' her mum said, tears springing to her eyes, 'I can't bear to think of you as a woman, but here you are, all grown up and ready to take on the world.'

Mirela had to bite her tongue so she didn't say something she might regret. She didn't want to upset her mammy, not tonight after she'd gone to so much trouble, but she wasn't a woman, she was still only a young girl and she wanted to be excited about the life ahead of her and all the thrills that young love had to offer. She sighed and glanced again at her reflection. 'Thanks, mammy,' she said, 'should we go out now?'

Mirela had been to enough of these coming of age celebrations to know what to expect, and tonight would be no exception. As she and her mother stepped out of their trailer, it was to whoops and clapping and wolf whistles. The music was already cranked up and playing, a huge fire was crackling away, and the smell of meat cooking was thick in the air. Noticing some cousins she hadn't seen in a while, Mirela made a beeline for them and was soon wrapped up in hearing funny stories about what they'd been up to over the summer.

'Oh my god,' she said to her cousin Dana, 'you look so gorgeous, just like Madonna!'

Dana giggled, 'it's what I was going for,' she said, 'I'm hoping some nice boy will notice me tonight, that's for sure,' she leaned towards Mirela and whispered loudly, 'I've even padded my bra so I have boobies, did you notice?'

Mirela frowned, Dana was only 14 herself and already she was hoping for a betrothal. What was wrong with these people? 'Behave yourself, Dana,' she scolded, 'just have fun with the girls, there's plenty of time for all that nonsense.'

'Come on, come on, Mirela,' Bo Lee shouted above the din, 'it's your night, my daughter,' he turned to the large crowd of friends and relatives and yelled, 'let's dance, drink and be merry!'

'I'll catch up with you in a bit, Dana,' she said, making her way carefully across to where her dad was waiting, his arms open wide for a hug.

Mirela almost fell over when she saw who was standing right by his side however.

'Thanks for this, dad,' she said, smiling, 'but I'll not spend my birthday standing here with the men, I want to catch up with everybody. And like you said, it's *my* night tonight.'

Chrissy Lee stepped forward, leering at Mirela, eyeing her up and down, 'and so it is, girl, and I'll be accompanying you,' he said, holding out his hand.

Mirela stubbornly clamped her arms to her sides and glared at her father, 'I don't need any supervision, daddy, but if *he* insists on following me around, then I'm not to be touched.'

Unbelievably, Bo Lee winked at Chrissy, 'I told you she needed taming, boy, worse than that filly you thought you could master last week.'

Mirela wanted to cry as she watched her dad and her wretched cousin laugh out loud as they compared her to an untamed horse. She felt even worse as her dad walked away, still laughing, leaving her alone with Chrissy. Well, she didn't intend to have any kind of courtship whatsoever with him, so she decided just to do her own thing and if he followed, he followed, she'd simply ignore him.

Chrissy had no intention of allowing that to happen. As Mirela scowled then turned to walk away, he grabbed her shoulder roughly and pulled her back round to him.

'Don't think about showing me up, cousin,' he said, 'I'm to marry you and that's all there is to it. But if it's a fight you want, then you'll have one because I'll not be belittled in front of my family, and you will act like a lady, you hear me?'

Mirela shrugged him off, but he'd hurt her and now she was wary, 'look, Chrissy,' she said, 'I don't want to offend you, or show you up, but this is my 15th birthday party and I want to enjoy it. Please, can I spend some time with you later? I want to go speak with my aunties for a while.'

Chrissy silently stared at her for a few moments before speaking, 'fine, have it your way,' he said, a grin spreading across his face, 'but you will marry me, Mirela,' he looked around and then laughed, 'from what I've heard you're the only one left who's unsullied, so we need to get it arranged fast before you fall like the others have. Meet me by the showers at 10.00 and I'll show you what it's like to be kissed by a man.'

Mirela felt nothing but disgust as she walked away. Her whole body was shaking with temper. She knew what unsullied meant, but surely he can't have been talking about her other cousins, they were so young. There was no way she would be meeting that creep at ten o'clock or any other time. An idea was forming in her head and the more she thought about it, the more appealing it seemed. She would sleep with Patti and be done with it. She'd no longer be pure, so Chrissy would leave her alone, and she would be sealing her love with Patti. She knew he wanted to, as their canoodling in his caravan had been getting more amorous just lately, and both knew it was only a matter of time before they could no longer stop themselves. The only problem with her plan would be her parents. They would most likely disown her, as would the whole of the community.

The rest of the party was fun, Mirela danced with her friends and sat singing round the fire, but all the while she kept her eye out for Chrissy. He was friends with the other twin, Michael James, and the two of them were drinking together over by the beer tent but it was clear they were keeping an eye on her too. As was tradition, Bina, hobbled across to bless Mirela with happiness and many babies and the other girls laughed to watch her blush and pull her hands away. But it was all good fun and Mirela had to admit, she had enjoyed herself despite the fact that her Patti wasn't there to share it. In an ideal world she would have shared tonight with her real boyfriend, her real love, and not be worrying constantly about a thug that she hated. At half past nine, she went looking for her mother. Her plan was to feign a headache so her mum would tell her to go back to the trailer for a lie down, and she'd avoid having to meet her creepy cousin.

'Poor thing,' Violet said, immediately feeling her daughter's forehead, 'you do seem a bit hot, girl, I think you should call it a night and go have a lie down. Go on back to the van, Mirela, and I'll let them all know you're not well. I'll not be far behind you, the men are getting rowdy as usual and they won't want us women around for long.'

Mirela kept to the shadows as she made her way back to the trailer, making sure no one could see her. She smiled to herself as she saw the porch light shining outside her home. She had outwitted the fools. But she was wrong, and it was too late to do anything about it now as Chrissy Lee stepped out from behind a cart.

'Ah, we meet again, Mirela, so you thought you'd give me the slip, did you?' he slurred, clearly drunk already, 'or is this what you wanted, my feisty cousin, a dark corner so we could be completely alone?'

Mirela tried to move past him, 'Chrissy, I'm sorry, but I'm not well. My mother is following behind me, we're going back to the trailer.'

'Wrong!' Chrissy announced gleefully, 'my friend, Michael James is currently keeping your mother company, asking her for stories from the old days, and you know what she's like once she gets into all that, so it's just you and me. Now then, what to do.'

'Please, Chrissy,' Mirela begged, but Chrissy suddenly grabbed her and threw her against a trailer.

'Shut up,' he demanded as he pinned her arms and forced his mouth onto hers.

Mirela felt hot and faint. She couldn't move as her cousin thrust his tongue down her throat. It was disgusting and made her feel sick. Then, as he started to groan and push himself into her, Mirela allowed herself to slip to the floor. She hoped he might see that he'd hurt her and be scared enough to walk away, but no, Chrissy fell down on top of her, and this time he held a hand across her mouth so she couldn't cry out as he groped her breasts and then violently grabbed at her private parts. Mirela wanted to die as she felt rough fingers plunging painfully inside of her. All she could do was pray silently that he wouldn't rape her and that he'd stop soon.

'There,' Chrissy said, suddenly sitting up and rubbing his hand through his hair, 'that settles things now, you're mine and I'm yours. Get up and go clean yourself up, Mirela, we're done here.'

Astounded, Mirela scrambled to her feet and without looking back she ran, carrying her shoes, to her own trailer. She was almost blinded by tears as she burst sobbing through the doors, and then straight to the bathroom. They had the luxury of running water in their sink, so she filled it as she stripped off her clothes and then began scrubbing her body with the soap and flannel. She couldn't believe what had just happened to her, and when she told her parents, they would at last see that she could never marry Chrissy now. But she was in for an even bigger shock.

'Oh, baby,' her mother soothed after she'd cried to her and told her the whole story. The whole story apart from the most vile part. 'I'm sorry he frightened you like that. Bloody Chrissy is like a bull in a china shop, but he meant well, baby girl. I'm sure he didn't mean you any harm.'

'He meant well?' Mirela shouted, pulling herself from her mother's arms, 'did you not just hear what I said? He hurt me, mammy, and it was disgusting! He's the most vile person I've ever met in my life, it was horrible.'

'It's just our way, Mirela,' her mum said, 'that's what happens, it's the way men court girls. Grab them, kiss them, make them their own, it's like staking a claim that's all, it's…'

Mirela didn't want to hear any more. If her own mother felt this way, then surely her dad would too. She could barely believe that her own parents would expect her to be put through something so traumatic. 'Well, he's a pig, and I hate him,' she yelled, 'and I won't put up with that, I won't.'

She ran to her bedroom and sobbed into her pillow for a long time before sleep finally took her and gave her some respite from the horrors her mind was replaying.

Chapter 11

Patti could hear that his dad was raging at someone over the phone. He had meant to set off to Derby at 9.00am and now he was screaming that he'd be late. It wasn't yet time for Patti to set off to work and he wanted a cup of tea before he went, so he risked his dad's wrath by joining him in the kitchen.

'I'll fucking kill him!' Pat screamed as he slammed the phone down, 'fucking gypsy king? Fucking snake more like!'

'What's up, dad?' Patti asked, his ears pricking at the mention of gypsies.

'Bo fucking Lee, that's what's up,' Pat yelled, 'I'm going to look a right cunt going down there to the lads now, aren't I?'

Patti felt a sudden sickness in the pit of his stomach, 'what's he done, dad?' he asked.

'I fucking told him yesterday that I was buying half a dozen jack hammers and all those angle grinders off Mick Keenan today. I've just phoned that simpleton, Keenan, only to be told that Bo fucking Lee went in first thing and bought the bastard lot! I'm gonna see that cunt dead, just watch me.'

'And did you need them?' Patti asked, feeling stupid the minute the words had left his mouth.

'Well of course I fucking needed them,' Pat shouted, 'half the lads already down there are waiting for them. What do you think *they* will use, their fucking fingers? Fuck this!' he yelled, 'tell your mother I'm off. I'll have to pay top whack now because of that pikey cunt.'

Patti was shaking, he didn't need this. His dad and Mirela's at war and clouding their relationship, it just couldn't happen, and what if his dad really did go after Bo Lee, what then? Both were hard men, and neither afraid of a fight. This could be disastrous and Mirela couldn't find out, he decided. He was just glad he hadn't been at the scrap yard when Bo had been and got the goods otherwise his dad would have blamed him too. Feeling too sick to have a cup of tea now, he decided to grab a pint of milk from the fridge instead and set off to work. It was August, and the heat, even at this time of the morning was searing. He knew Mirela would be joining him this morning and that the tatty caravan would be like a greenhouse by the time he got there so he stopped at the shop on the way, and bought some cold drinks to keep up there. He could keep them cool in Mick's fridge until he needed them.

He was pissed off too with Danielle, she had been practically blackmailing him because she was so jealous about the amount of time he was spending with Mirela, always threatening to tell mam or dad about his sneaking around. They both knew now though, that he had a girlfriend, so she could do what she liked, still, it irked him as he and his sister had always been so close. Thing was, now there was this animosity between his dad and Bo Lee, he would definitely have to keep her identity a secret. The lot of them would go apeshit if they knew he was cavorting with the enemy, so he guessed he'd still have to keep Danielle onside after all.

Patti finally arrived at work with the weight of the world on his shoulders. Mick Keenan, as usual, made a beeline for him as he walked through the wrought iron gates,

'Come on, young 'un,' he shouted, 'we've a load of lead coming in this morning and I need some space clearing in the lock up. Thieving bastards probably had it off a church roof, so I don't want to leave it lying around to be nicked off me.'

'I'll just put these drinks in your fridge, Mick,' Patti said, 'and then I'll get straight on it.'

'What's up with your miserable boat race?' Mick asked, 'lost a sixpence and found a penny?'

'Nah,' Patti said, 'just had some shit off my dad this morning. Bo Lee bought that demo stuff he was after and he's not happy.'

Mick laughed, 'it's just business, lad, nowt personal, and your dad knows I always see him right. He'll be back.' He was about to walk away but then called back, 'isn't it Bo Lee's lass that you've been knocking about with?'

Patti stopped in his tracks. Mick was sneaky, he knew that, but what if he said something to either of them? 'Mick, it's meant to be a secret. You won't say anything will you?'

Mick winked and laughed, 'your secret's safe with me, lad. Your dad's a good fella, and I have my own reasons for getting one up on Bo Lee. Why d'ya think he got the dodgy demolition gear and not your dad?'

It suddenly dawned on Patti what had happened, 'well why didn't you just tell my dad about it?' he asked, puzzled, 'then he wouldn't have been so mad.'

'Like I said, I got my reasons,' Mick said, 'now come on, let's have some graft out of you. The sooner you're done, the sooner you can sneak off to that little love nest you think I don't know about.'

Patti blushed and then grinned, 'thanks, Mick,' he said, 'and don't worry, I'll do a good job.'

It was around half past one when Patti finally got done and he was down at his own little van, washing his hands when he saw Mirela heading towards him. Glancing around to check it was all tidy, he smiled at how it was coming along. He'd managed to sneak some cushions and blankets from his mum's airing cupboard the day before, and now the seating area looked nice and cosy. All they needed now was a new bit of carpet, some curtains, and it would look almost homely. He was surprised therefore, when Mirela stepped in and didn't seem to notice.

'Oh, Patti, I'm so fed up of everything,' she said, throwing herself into his arms, 'I hate my life, I hate it!'

'Hey, hey, what on earth is wrong,' Patti asked, kissing her forehead and stroking her hair, 'come on, let's sit down and you can tell me what's happened,' as he stroked her hair back, he noticed the red marks on the back of her neck, 'Mirela, who's hurt you? What are these marks?' He asked, anger bubbling up in him, 'what the fuck has happened?'

Mirela burst into tears as she told Patti all about her birthday and the disgusting treatment she'd had from Chrissy Lee.

'But worse than that,' she sobbed, 'my mammy and daddy seem to think that that's normal, and I should take it with a pinch of salt. They said that it's all a part of courtship and that all the other girls accept it. Patti, I hate them all!'

Patti remained silent until she'd finished talking, but he was livid. How dare that bastard lay his hands on her, hurt her? And what kind of parents were Mirela's to put up with it. He knew for a fact that if some lad had ever so much as touched his sister, his mam and dad would be round at his house and battering his door down to get at the creep. He knew Chrissy Lee, mainly from seeing him around the pubs near his house. He used to drink outside them with the other Gypsies, always gobby and loud, trying to intimidate the usual punters as they went in. But like most bullies, he was only like this when he had a crowd around him.

'I will fucking kill him!' Patti swore, 'as god is my witness, I'll fucking murder him, Mirela, I'll do time for the bastard!'

'No, Patti,' Mirela cried, 'you can't. There are too many of them, cousins, friends, and even those that hate him would have to have his back, it's the way they work. There's nothing I can do other than stay away from him and hope my dad sees how stupid it is to force me to be with him.'

Surprised by the rage inside of him, Patti tried to calm down. Mirela was clearly upset, the last thing she needed was someone else giving her grief. 'Okay, it's okay, baby,' he said, hugging her closely, 'but we have to do something. You can't be afraid every time you go home, it's not right.'

'I'm not afraid, Patti,' she said, 'not as long as I have you. I don't care what they think, they can't control me, and I won't have it.'

Patti had never felt such love and it scared him, but at the same time it made him feel different. As if he suddenly had a great responsibility and he knew that whatever happened, this girl would always come first. Before him, and before anybody else. He started to kiss her, tenderly at first, but as Mirela responded, clearly aroused, he felt the now familiar stirrings within himself. Rather than pulling away, as she had in the past, Mirela pushed herself onto Patti so they were both laid on the new blankets and cushions. Soon, they were entwined and grabbing desperately at each other's clothing.

'Mirela,' Patti whispered, his voice hoarse, 'I won't be able to stop soon…'

'Hush, Patti,' she said, 'hush.'

When they had finished, Patti felt an overwhelming urge to cry. He bit his lip as he lay naked, still wrapped tightly around Mirela.

'Are you okay, baby?' He asked.

'I'm more than okay,' Mirela answered, smiling at him, 'I love you, Patti.' She kissed him softly, and then Patti couldn't hold it in any longer.

'I love you too,' he whispered, his tears falling onto her cheeks. 'I don't know why I'm crying,' he tried to laugh, 'but I know I love you, and I want us to be together for ever.'

Mirela hadn't been his first, he'd had his way with two girls before her, but she was definitely the first that he'd had feelings for, and for some reason, he felt reborn. As if this were the first day of the rest of his life. It didn't matter that every possible obstacle was already in their way, and no doubt there'd be more hurdles, all that mattered was that somehow, this girl would be his, and nothing anyone might say or do would stop it from happening.

Chapter 12

Violet looked in on her daughter who was still sleeping, and yearned for the old days when the child depended on her for everything. Times when her days were filled with the joys of teaching Mirela the ways of their world. After her initial period of depression, she'd loved being a mother. She remembered her child's squeals of delight as they baked bread together, or laughed as they hung out their sheets on a blustery day. She sighed now, accepting that this girl was no longer a child, but a young woman soon to be married off to a Lee man. She hoped and prayed that Mirela would find some happiness, would find some way to make it work, just as she had. Not that happiness had played a big part in Violet's life, but there had been moments when she'd given thanks for the life she had, and knew she could certainly have done worse. For as big and hard as he was, Bo Lee, had never harmed a woman.

'Is she out of her pit yet?' Bo shouted as he came into the trailer for a mug of tea, 'I'm taking her with me to Leeds later on, one of the lads is in need of a pick up truck, and there's a mush over there that owes us a favour.'

'She said she's not feeling too good and wants to have a lie in,' Violet told him, 'I think we should leave her be today, Bo, she might be coming down with something.'

'That girl is suffering from a stubborn streak and nothing else,' her husband yelled, 'I have our Brendan chewing my head off about when the wedding will happen. Chrissy won't wait forever, Violet, it's not right.'

Brendan was Bo Lee's brother, and as much of a pig as his son Chrissy. He had always taunted Bo about how he should have left his wife years ago so he could have a son, and Violet hated him for it. She'd never have another child and it wasn't her fault. Mirela had been a miracle, after the damage she'd suffered after being trampled by the horse, but all the doctors had been clear that another viable pregnancy would never be on the cards.

'Just give her a bit of time, Bo,' Violet said, 'it's a shock to her that's all. And she is actually unwell, she's got a temperature too.'

'Why?' Bo said, 'why is it a shock? She's known since the day she could talk who she would marry. I knew she should never have gone to school, the fucking gorgers filling her head with shite!'

Violet was about to lose her temper and didn't want to. Mirela had heard too many arguments just lately, and it wasn't like her to take to her bed without reason.

'Just stop it, Bo!' She yelled, closing the bedroom door softly as she walked into the living area, 'I said she's not well, and that's that. She can go out with you another day.'

'Time was she'd leap at the chance to come with me,' he yelled back, 'now all she does is clean and mop up after the other women. All she's doing is putting off the day she has to do it for herself, and it's no good for her. Don't bother with my tea, I'm off.'

Violet watched as her husband stormed angrily away towards his group of cronies and she shook her head sadly. Putting off the inevitable is what she herself had been doing if truth be told. She always knew of course that the day would come when her daughter was married off and presented with her own home, but she'd hoped that by then she and Bo would have a happier marriage, and that she'd be looking forward to being part of a couple again without the responsibility of a child. She just thought she had more time. More time to be a mother, because what after that? She was no wife in the ordinary sense. Bo would always have to take another woman for all that business, because all there was for Violet to do was cook and clean and be there to listen when it was required. Her grim thoughts were broken as Mirela came out of her room.

'Has he gone?' She asked, 'only I really don't want to go with him, mammy, especially as Chrissy will be there too.'

'He's gone,' Violet said, 'but, my girl, you can't keep putting off getting to know Chrissy. It will only make things worse for you. Come sit down, I'll make you some sweet tea, are you still feeling a bit off?'

Mirela nodded, 'I'll have that and then I might go for a little walk, see if I feel better. I might go and help Mary Jane for a bit too. She's making some new curtains and I said I'd give a hand.'

Violet got up to make some drinks, 'you've been doing a lot of helping her lately, girl, and your dad's getting a bit lairy about it. You've hardly spent any time with him recently, and don't blame Chrissy being there because he was away all last week.'

'I thought you'd be pleased I'm learning the ways of being a traveler's wife, mammy,' Mirela said with a hint of sarcasm. 'I mean cooking, cleaning and baby minding is far better for me than educating myself or reading a book, is it not? According to you and daddy of course.'

'Mind your tongue, Mirela,' Violet scolded as she passed a cup and saucer towards her, 'and if it's housework you're yearning for, there's plenty to do here, so don't be all day. Oh, and if you see the other twin, Michael James, tell him your dad wants him to drop this off with the landlord at the Brown Cow.' She passed her the envelope Bo had left on the side, 'and it's important, so don't forget.'

Violet sat down heavily when her daughter left. This situation had no happy ending at all. If she forced Mirela's hand, her daughter hated her, and if she fought for the girl, her husband hated her. This was a battle she could never win no matter what the result, and she knew in that moment that happiness had simply never been on the cards for her, she had surely been cursed for some reason, and nothing she did could alter that.

***

Mirela was annoyed she'd have to actually call at the twin's trailer. Although Mary Jane was lovely enough, she didn't like Michael James, he was a bit creepy, not a bit like his sister who was kind and funny. Also, Mirela was sure that he knew all about what Chrissy Lee had done to her the night of her birthday party. Mary Jane wouldn't mind a bit that she had no intention of helping her with her sewing, but she wondered how she'd manage to get away and not have her mammy find out. As she walked around to their trailer, it was actually Della who provided the perfect opportunity.

'Oh hello, Mirela,' Della panted as she caught up with her, 'I'm just on my way to see the twins. My Daisy has the summer flu again and I can't leave her for too long, she's got a high fever, bless her heart, I'm going to strip a chicken to make her some soup. I was going to ask Mary Jane if she'd post this letter for me. She said she was going to town.'

'Give it to me and you get back to Daisy, I have a letter to post for my mammy so I can take it,' Mirela said, thinking quickly, 'is it to your mammy in Ireland?'

'Oh, bless you,' Della said, 'and it is. She's not well herself so it'll cheer her up, I'll get back to Daisy and the little ones then if you're sure.'

'No problem at all,' Mirela said, 'and give my love to Daisy will you.'

Della ran back to her own trailer leaving Mirela with two envelopes now, but her escape from the site was made easier. If Della said anything to her mammy now, everyone would just assume she was being helpful, as always.

'And can you ask your brother if he'll sort this one out for my dad?' she said after explaining to Mary Jane about Della. 'I have to go and watch the kiddies for her now while she sorts Daisy out,' she continued, 'so I can't really help you with the curtains today.'

The older girl laughed, 'think nothing of it, sweetie,' she said but then leaned a little closer, 'I'm not supposed to say, Mirela,' she said softly, 'but Chrissy Lee suspects that you're up to something untoward. He's asked my brother to keep his eye on you. Now I don't know what you're up to, but I'd watch myself if I were you.'

Mirela was stunned. She thought she'd been so careful, but god knows what would happen if Michael James started following her. She could feel her cheeks redden as she spoke next.

'Thanks for telling me, Mary Jane,' she said before giving her a pleading look, 'I'm really not up to anything. Just trying to stay away from our trailer as much as I can, but please look out for me, will you? I mean, if the boys are saying things about me, just try shut them up. I can do without gossip getting back to my daddy, as if things aren't bad enough at home.'

Mary Jane placed a hand on her shoulder, 'I'll do what I can, darling, I promise, but do be careful, this is a hard life to buck up against.'

Mirela was shaking as she sneaked away from the site and she could feel her world collapsing in on her. She had more secrets than even Patti knew, but she realized she would have to open up to him now, if she had any hope at all of future happiness.

Chapter 13

Patti wasn't pleased. He'd had the shock of his life earlier when Bo Lee's truck had pulled into the scrap yard, and there, sitting right beside him was Chrissy Lee. Pressing his face up against the window of Mick's cabin, he could see clearly who it was.

'Fucking wanker!' He growled, making his way to the door, 'let's see how brave he is when it's not a young girl who confronts him.'

'Don't even think about it, lad,' Mick Keenan said, grabbing Patti by the arm, 'you stay in here and I'll go out and deal with those two. But I know the score with that Chrissy, and trust me, you'd need an army, lad. There's more than one way to skin a cat, so stay put.'

Patti was shaking with anger, but he did as Mick had told him, and watched quietly from the portacabin. He didn't regret telling his boss about what Chrissy had done to Mirela, but he wished he had stressed more the importance of keeping his secret. He just hoped Mick liked him enough to cover his back. Within five minutes, the gypsies had jumped back into the pick up and drove away.

'Was it about those dodgy angle grinders and stuff?' Patti asked, 'did they come here to start with you?'

Mick laughed, 'not at all, lad,' he said, 'he'll have only had those for bloody half an hour, he was passing them on. No, they're on their way to Leeds for some truck and they might have to hide it away up here for a few weeks when they bring it back.'

'They off to nick one?' Patti asked, wondering why they'd have to hide it.

'Let's just say they are retrieving it from someone who ought to know better than to owe a gypsy king a couple of thousand pounds for too long.'

By the time Mirela arrived, he had calmed down, and he marveled at the happiness he felt just watching her walk towards him. His heart raced and he broke into a smile every time he even thought about her.

'You're a sight for sore eyes,' he declared as he put his arms around her and planted a kiss on her lips. 'Mick's given us a fridge and some more cups and stuff, so you go down to the van and I'll be there in ten minutes. I've connected the gas bottle up as well, so you can make us both a cuppa.'

Mirela laughed and kissed him back, 'proper little housewife you are, Patti,' she giggled, 'don't be too long though because I only have a couple of hours before they start to miss me. And I have things I need to tell you.'

Patti went back into Mick's portacabin and carried on adding up all the receipts he'd been given, 'I'll soon have this done,' he said, 'and then is it alright if I go down to the caravan for an hour? Mirela doesn't have long today.'

'Here, lad, I'll finish those off,' Mick said, scooting his chair up to the desk, 'I remember what young love's like, son, you get down to your lass, but I'll need you up here this afternoon before those cars get delivered.'

Cars were the main part of Mick's operation, and not asking any questions was just as important. Patti knew that most cars used in Bradford's robberies were brought up here to be scrapped, and Mick needed them stripping down and VIN numbers welding off within hours of them arriving, others, the ones that were too hot, were taken elsewhere and stored in a big barn where they were cut and shut and sold on in different counties.

'Don't worry,' Patti said, 'I'll be here, are the other lads coming in to help?'

Mick nodded as he put his glasses on and got on with the receipts, 'just for an hour or so, lad, but long enough to help you get them all stripped down, I'll see you in a bit.'

Mirela was sitting on a wooden crate outside the van when he got down there, her hair flowing out behind her in the breeze. Her beauty almost took his breath away, but instead of the happy smile he was used to being greeted with, he noticed she looked sad.

'Baby, what's wrong?' Patti asked as he sat down with her, 'I thought you'd be happy today, with your dad being off in Leeds. He was up here before he went.' He decided not to mention that Chrissy had been there too. No point in causing her more misery than she already had in her life.

'I am happy,' Mirela said, 'but Patti, I've been keeping a secret, and now I'm scared to tell you.'

Patti stared at her, his heart suddenly feeling heavy, 'Mirela, there's nothing you can't tell me, baby, nothing. Now just spit it out, come on.'

'Okay then,' Mirela said, her chin jutting out as she turned to look at him, 'I've missed my monthly visitor.'

Patti was confused, 'your monthly what?'

'My visitor. You know, Patti, the thing that happens to girls every month?'

It suddenly dawned on him, 'your... your period you mean?'

Mirela nodded then hung her head and started to cry, 'I'm so sorry, Patti, I don't know what to do. I'll be disowned now anyway, so I don't have to worry about that, but oh, it's all too much. They have spies watching out for me, my daddy will kill me for sure, I hate my life! And to drag you into it too, I'm sorry, Patti, honest I am, I mean we have only been together for two bloody minutes. I'll understand if you want to call it a day.'

Patti remained silent for a few moments, the enormity of the situation sinking in. He thought about what she was saying, giving him an out if he wanted it, but even as the thought crossed his mind, he knew that he didn't. He then smiled and shook his head softly, before grabbing hold of Mirela's shoulders. 'Look, baby, I love you, and you love me. If you're pregnant, then so be it. We can be happy, we can be a little family, don't get upset, baby, we will work it out, we will.'

He actually had no idea if or how they could work it out, but he suddenly felt fiercely protective of both Mirela and the baby she could be carrying. His baby. He hugged her closely to him and kissed the top of her head, 'please don't cry, Mirela, just know that I love you more than anything in the world, and I'll come up with a plan, I promise you.'

Chapter 14

Mick Keenan sighed as he watched the young Gypsy girl walk by his portacabin, hand in hand with young Patti King. He took off his glasses and scratched his head as he stood to look out of the window. He liked Patti, he was a lot like his old man in some ways. A sharp mind and the ability to turn his hand to any situation at any given moment. He smiled as he pictured Patti's face whenever he was being shown how to do something. The boy had a habit of slightly sticking his tongue out as he concentrated on something, determined to be able to do it himself without any further instruction. Just what Mick needed in his line of work. Show them once, then expect to be able to leave them to it. When Big Pat had more or less ordered him to take on his kid, Mick had only agreed at the time as the work had been piling up, and he'd intended on keeping him for a few weeks and then setting a real grafter on, but the truth was, Patti was a natural grafter himself. He also knew how to keep his mouth shut and in his line of business that was crucial, so, all in all, he was a good fit.

This thing he had going though, with Bo Lee's daughter, was sure to end in tears. Or something much worse. Mick's mantra had always been, *know your enemy,* but of course young Patti couldn't possibly know what he was getting himself in to. Parents protected their kids from all that shit until they were old enough to be brought into it, and Big Pat didn't think his lad had either the balls, or the sense to be told what was what just yet.

Mick knew though, he knew everything. There wasn't a crook in Bradford that he hadn't been personally involved with in one way or another over the years. And the thing about crooks was, they weren't afraid to talk. They were always happy to let slip what someone else was up to, and often bragged if they'd managed to get one over on someone. That hadn't been the case with Big Pat King and Bo Lee though. They kept what was private, private. It had been some other slimy bastard, years later, who told Mick all about their beef. And it was something he'd kept to himself all this time, something he would never dare bring up to either man, not least because there had been a tenuous truce of sorts between the two of them for years now.

Not for long though, Mick said to himself as he came away from the window, not comfortable watching the young lovebirds snogging by the gates. When all this with Patti and Mirela blew up – which it would, Mick knew that all past grievances would resurface, and then a price would certainly have to be paid. He paled as he thought back to what had happened sixteen years ago, and wondered how he himself would cope if he'd been in Bo Lee's shoes that day. Everyone knew that the Gypsy King had been thrilled that at last, his wife was pregnant with a son. He and Violet had been trying ever since their wedding day and it had finally been confirmed by the old gypsy seer. There had been parties and celebrations when the gender had been announced, and gypsies from all over the country had visited with gifts and to toast the impending new arrival.

Who could have imagined though the tragedy that would follow the very day that Pat King had turned up at the site, looking for Bo Lee to offer him some financial opportunity that would earn him thousands of pounds. The story that Mick heard was that Big Pat had been the one who had opened the gate of the paddock, just as the wild horse had reared up and galloped away. The men had screamed at Pat to secure the field, but he'd failed to do it in time and the horse got away, trampling poor Violet Lee in its' path.

Bo Lee had been too lost in his grief when the baby was gone, and especially so when he learned his wife might never again bear a child, but he'd never forgotten that his pain was essentially down to Pat King. Big Pat had never accepted this, he saw it as a tragic accident, but since then, the men had only ever been civil with each other if they had to be, and their long standing friendship had ended that day. Pat had been wise enough at the time not to let it be known that his own wife was also pregnant. If Bo Lee had known that, his pain would have been tenfold.

Mick shook himself out of his somber thoughts as Patti came into the cabin. He smiled, 'everything alright, son?'

Patti shook his head, his face pale and drawn, 'not one fucking bit alright, Mick,' he said, 'I don't know what we're going to do.'

'Shut the door, lad, and tell me what's up. And listen, I know in the beginning I teased you a bit and I let slip to your dad that you had a bird up here, but I promise you, Patti, what you tell me won't leave this room, you're a good kid.'

Mick's face also paled as he listened to what Patti told him. If he was afraid of what was to come before, he was definitely terrified now. For Patti, not himself.

'Patti, you need to think seriously about this,' he said, 'before you make any decisions, lad. She's only fifteen, and that would be hard enough for any girl, but for a gypsy it's, it's…' Mick tried to think of a suitable word, 'it's a fucking life sentence, son. They'd all shun her, the lot of 'em, not just the ones in Bradford, I'm talking about pikeys from all over England, and that's besides what her dad will do to her. Can't she go somewhere to get rid of it?'

'What? You mean like an abortion?' Patti asked, in horror, 'she's a catholic, Mick, and so am I. No, there's no chance of that. We don't give a fuck about them disowning her or whatever, she's better off without 'em, we intend on keeping the baby, we just need a plan that's all.'

Mick knew that like most of the families he mixed with, the King family were all very proud of their Catholic beliefs, and even though going to church had only ever been something they did as young children, just to be able to get into the better schools – according to Big Pat anyway, abortion was one of the biggest sins, and unlike all the others such as no sex before marriage, honouring thy father and thy mother, not telling lies etc, it was the one sin that couldn't be committed. Patti would know that his mother would forgive most things, even murder if it was justified, but getting rid of a baby? His life wouldn't be worth living.

Mick shook his head, 'it's your life, Patti, I'm just pointing out what's to come, but you'll do what you want to do anyway. I just hope that whatever plan you're thinking of, it doesn't involve living in that caravan down the yard, because much as I like you, son, I can not get involved in any of this. I'm not lying when I say that Bo Lee will fucking end me if I do.'

'But we'll need some help, Mick,' Patti pleaded, 'I thought you were on my side.'

Mick thought for a moment, wondering if he should tell Patti a secret of his own. Not about the accident, that wasn't his story to tell, but about the thing he'd kept buried for over 17 years, the thing that made him hate Bo Lee. He took a deep breath and sighed before deciding to lay out all his own cards.

'I was in your exact shoes, lad, a long time ago,' Mick finally said, 'in fact it was the very same fucking family if you want the truth. Violet Lee, Mirela's mum, used to be Violet Hearne, and she was the most stunning bird I've ever laid eyes on in my life.'

Mick smiled as he watched Patti's eyes widen, but he carried on unburdening himself, 'I was only 18 at the time, and she was about the same age, but anyway, we were in love and swore we'd run away together. Just like you and your lass there. Trouble was, she was engaged to Bo Lee, and had been since she was about 12. Even though I begged her to stay with me, she wanted the life he offered more. That and the fact she was too scared to buck against tradition, not like your lass.'

'Jesus Christ, Mick,' Patti said, 'as if you never mentioned it when you knew who I was seeing, so what happened? She just dump you and marry him?'

Mick nodded, 'he never found out about us, ever. Violet must have kept it quiet too, so that's a good thing or I'd probably be hobbling about like fucking bent Stanley by now. But anyway, like I said, that's ancient history, and I did hope, when I first saw you and her together, that you might have broken the mould, and got away with her. But not like this,' he shook his head again, 'I can't see beyond what Bo Lee will do to you, lad, you're going to have to fuck off, and by fuck off I mean get right out of dodge, as far away as you can get. I mean it, he'll kill you.'

What Mick didn't tell Patti was that he'd also had a fling with his mother, Maureen, and that she and Violet Lee had almost come to blows over him, but that was a story best forgotten. No point in upsetting the lad any more than necessary.

Patti sighed and sat down, 'I can't think, Mick,' he said as he hung his head, running his fingers through his hair, 'you let her go. That Violet. You gave up, well I won't. I just have to find a way.'

Chapter 15

Mirela stared at her naked body in the long mirror on the back of her wardrobe door. She was sure she could see a change in her shape, and she turned sideways as she ran a hand over her belly. A definite small bulge, she was sure of it, but she could only be 8 or 9 weeks at most. The last few weeks had been difficult to manage, and she knew it was only a matter of time before she and Patti got caught sneaking around together. The 'big plan' hadn't yet been hatched, and all their conversations lately had been about the reality of running away together. Yes, Patti could probably get another job somewhere else, but she couldn't, and where would they live? They could never afford their own house, and anyway, they'd probably always need to be on the move because her dad would never stop until he hunted them down, and what kind of life was that for a baby?

Mirela knew that Patti was a bit of a dreamer if truth be told. He had lots of big ideas, but no real way of implementing them. Even though she was younger and less experienced in the ways of the world, she knew that in the end, it would be down to her to make this work out. She had already been thinking about enlisting an ally – someone she could tell the truth to, someone she could trust, and right now, convinced that everyone would soon notice her extra weight, she knew that today was as good as any to go talk to Mary Jane.

 Of all the people that she'd grown up with, Mary Jane had always been the kindest to her, always looked out for her and made sure she was alright. Daisy Wright, Della's daughter would have understood too, she felt, but she might let something slip to Della, and then her mother would definitely find out. No, Mary Jane was about the only person in the world, besides Patti, that she could trust. Positive she was doing the right thing, Mirela quickly dressed before she lost her nerve and changed her mind.

Half an hour later, sitting, sipping tea from bone China, Mirela was having second thoughts. She watched as her friend busied herself tidying away all the scraps of material that had been laid out on the seating area. Unlike her twin brother, Mary Jane wasn't so bad looking. She'd never be described as a stunner, and that was probably why she didn't have a husband herself just yet, but she was a good, kind girl and that's exactly what Mirela needed right now. But what if she'd read her all wrong? What if her friend's loyalties would lay with her brother and Chrissy?

'So,' Mary Jane said, smiling as she sat down, 'what is it that's having you sitting here like a bag of nerves, child? Nothing is that bad you know.'

'Oh, it really is, you have no idea,' Mirela said before looking nervously around, 'your brother isn't here is he?'

Mary Jane looked serious for a moment, 'No, Michael James is off somewhere with your betrothed, but I'm guessing it's he you want to talk about, am I right?'

Mirela was shocked, was she that easy to read? 'well, yes and no,' she said, trying to think of an easy way to explain the mess she was in, 'look, Mary Jane, can I really trust you? I mean really. Because what I'm about to tell you is no small thing.'

Mary Jane leaned forward and touched Mirela's hand, 'baby girl, you can trust me with anything, but if it makes it any easier, I already know you've been seeing a gorger. Is that your secret?'

'How?' Mirela spluttered, 'how do you know that? Does anyone else know? Oh my god, Mary Jane, how long have you known?'

'I keep my ear close to the ground,' Mary Jane said, 'and because nobody really notices me, I hear things that I shouldn't, but don't worry, I keep these things to myself.' She squeezed Mirela's hand, 'but I should warn you, it's from Michael James and Chrissy Lee that I heard it. They've both known for some time and from what I hear, they are just trying to find out who it is before they go to your father about it.'

Mirela felt sick. Not the sick that she'd been feeling every morning for the last four weeks, but a great, overwhelming urge to vomit her insides out. She burst into tears and then poured her heart out to her one friend, about Patti, the running around in secret, the scrap yard, and finally the pregnancy. There was no going back now.

Mary Jane was as white as a sheet as she allowed it all to sink in. She blessed herself with the sign of the cross and then clasped her hands together as if praying.

'Jesus, Mary and Joseph, Mirela! Are you sure? About the baby I mean?'

Mirela nodded, 'about nine weeks I think,' she said, subconsciously stroking her stomach, 'but I thought we had more time, more time to plan, but now that they know…' her voice trailed off as she imagined with horror the things Chrissy Lee would do to her if he knew the full truth. Her father would be horrified for sure, and very angry, but she knew he wouldn't harm her physically. He was nothing like the ugly cousin she was expected to marry.

Mary Jane stood up and paced the trailer in silence. Mirela watched as her friend then poured out two fresh cups of tea.

'I'm guessing if my brother and Chrissy know, and I know, then others might too,' she finally said, 'so whatever you decide to do, it needs to be done quickly, Mirela, and listen, I know you don't hold with all this stuff, but the first thing I would do is go to see Bina. I know you're afraid of her, and she's an old hag, but Mirela she's gifted, she genuinely is. You need to see her.'

'And that's your advice?' Mirela asked, incredulously, 'go see the old fortune teller? For what? She can only confirm what I've already told you and that's if she has the gift at all. She can't help me!'

'She can, Mirela!' Mary Jane insisted, 'that's what she does. Trust me, girl, go see her and leave me to try think of something for you.'

What Mirela couldn't possibly know, as she trudged across the site towards Bina's trailer, was that the old seer already knew about part of the girl's predicament. She too kept her ear close to the ground. It paid for her to know secrets, in more ways than one. The men and women would often pay her handsomely with gold or cash for her words of wisdom and a peek into their future. Still, despite having such a stellar reputation, Mirela had her doubts, and it was in this frame of mind that she knocked at Bina's door.

'I wondered when you'd be paying me a visit,' the old hag cackled as she allowed Mirela inside, 'sit down, child, and I'll get my cards out.'

Mirela cringed as she edged her way to the sofa. Unlike most of the trailers on site, this was no show wagon. There were none of the modern trappings here, no Crown Derby proudly on display, and certainly no squeaky clean walls and surfaces. Bina was of a different generation, and a different way of life. She had been a roadside traveler for years, running water, gas and electricity were alien to her, and she'd rather skin a baby rabbit for supper than open up a pack of burgers.

'Here alright?' Mirela asked, her eyes trying to adjust to the dim light of an old oil lamp. 'I'm here for some advice, Bina…'

'I know what you're here for,' Bina snapped as she lit her stinky pipe, 'you haven't been sticking to your own kind, have you, girl?' She lay three tarot cards on the wooden crate that served as a coffee table, and pointed at one, the upright fool, 'changes are afoot, girl, and this gorger you've been sneaking around with, will be your downfall. New beginings are not always all they are cracked up to be.'

Mirela stared at Bina, aghast, it seemed she really did know her stuff. She automatically clutched at her belly, 'and the next one? What is that?'

Bina wasn't stupid and had long since learned how to read cues, and she knew how to think fast, 'That's the ace of cups, girl, and I think that's the real reason you are here.' Bina re-lit her pipe and scooped the remaining card up with the first two, 'I won't be reading any more for you girl,' she stabbed a bony finger towards Mirela's middle, 'that child will be born out of sin.' She let out another throaty cackle as she saw Mirela's reaction, 'the seed of the devil himself.'

Horrified, Mirela burst into tears, 'please, Bina, I beg you, tell me what to do, I'm so afraid.'

Bina stood up and started to bang her pipe on a window sill, 'two choices, gel, get rid of it, or run. Run as fast and as far as you can, and never stop. Now go, I don't want that curse you're carrying leaving it's mark in here, go on.' The woman threw open her trailer door.

Mirela ran blindly from Bina's caravan, tears streaming down her face. The old hag was evil, calling her baby like that, pure evil. But even so, she had been right about one thing, Mirela and Patti didn't have many choices available to them, and one of the two suggested was out of the question. Running seemed to be the only option left.

Chapter 16

Maureen King was in her element. The Brown Cow was in full swing, the drinks were flowing, music blaring and Big Pat was working away again.

'This is the life, eh, girls!' She yelled above the din to the Herson sisters as they all danced to the Reggae track now playing. 'It's about us this song, three little birds!'

The women laughed hysterically at Maureen's joke, 'well, it could be about me and our Kate,' Elaine spluttered, 'but it's a while since you've been a size ten, Mo. I mean, you must have really squeezed your fun and farce into that bleeding dress!'

'Very funny, Elaine,' Maureen said, 'I nearly fell off me bleeding platforms! And I'll have you know there's plenty of fellas who'd like to get a grip of my fun and farce.' It was said in good spirits of course. The Herson girls were known for how mental they were in a fight, and Maureen knew how to choose her friends. 'I'm off outside for a bit of air,' she panted, 'you coming? There's a load of blokes out there with their tops off, it's like a fucking oven in 'ere.'

The sisters declined and carried on dancing as Maureen made her way to the door. She smiled as two men immediately stood up and gestured for her to take a seat on the bench they'd been sitting at. 'There you go, Mrs King,' one of them said, 'can't have you wearing those pretty legs out can we.'

'Nice to see there are still some gentlemen left in this town,' Maureen purred as she fluttered her eyelashes. She could feel another few free drinks coming on as she spoke. She didn't know the men, but everybody knew who she was. Pat had seen to that, so that she was always safe and protected, but in Maureen's head it was a hinderance. It was almost impossible to go out on the pull these days. She took a seat on one of the benches and marvelled at the gorgeous weather they were having. An Indian summer, the newsreader had said on the telly, almost unheard of in October, but set to last for a few more days.

Lost in her thoughts she didn't see her son at first, but another bloke at the table nudged her, 'isn't that your lad, Maureen?' he said, 'looks like he's looking for someone.'

Maureen stood up and waved to get Patti's attention. She smiled but inside she was fuming. The little twat better not have come to the pub to pester her for money or she'd swing for him.

'Patti, love,' she called, 'I'm over here.'

Patti took in the scene of his mother done up to the nines, amid a group of six topless blokes and shook his head at her. 'Mam, we need to talk, it's urgent.'

Embarrassed, Maureen glanced around before laughing, 'well, spit it out then, son, what is it?' She desperately hoped it wasn't that big Pat was home early for some reason, 'come on,' she urged, 'there's a few gin and tonics in there with my name on, I don't have all day.'

Patti looked nervous as he leaned towards his mother, 'not here, mam, can we go home?'

'Are you kidding me, son?' Maureen laughed, 'no, we can't fucking go home, I've only just got here!' She turned to check if the men were listening to the exchange, 'kids, eh?' She laughed, flicking her hair back, 'bring 'em up to be independent, and still round me bleeding ankles!'

Grabbing hold of Patti's arm with one hand, and carefully retrieving her drink with the other, she steered her son through the group of customers out enjoying the sunshine, and led him to the edge of the street. 'What the fuck is wrong with you, Patti?' she hissed, 'showing me up, coming to the bleeding pub for me like a fucking bad husband! What is it?' As tipsy as she already was, Maureen couldn't help but notice how scared her boy looked, she softened her tone, 'Patti, you're scaring me now, love, what's up?'

There was a wall that belonged to a cottage next door to the pub, and Patti walked to that and sat down. 'Mam, I've fucked up, big time,' he said as Maureen joined him, 'I don't know where to start.'

Maureen was really scared now as she saw her son was crying. Her mind raced as different criminal scenarios popped into her head. The little fucker must have been caught on the rob.

'Look, son, no matter what you've done, even if the cops know about it, your dad can fix it. He has the best solicitor in Bradford on his payroll, now come on, tell me, it's not fucking drugs is it? Because we can forgive you anything but not that, son.'

Maureen's overriding emotion as she listened to her son as he poured his heart out, was first relief but then anger. After all she'd always told him about wearing a Johnny, he'd only gone and got a bird up the duff! And not just any bird, a fucking Pikey of all things! She wasn't completely heartless though, she was still his mam after all, and he needed her help.

'I'll pay, son,' she said, when he'd stopped talking, 'we'll go private to one of them posh clinics and get rid. It'll only take a couple of days, then, problem solved, and no one needs to know. But I tell you what, lad, in future, you wrap that bleeding pecker in plastic, I mean it!'

'Are you for fucking real, mam?' Patti spat, angrily, 'did you not just hear a word of what I said, or did you just pick out the bits you wanted, as usual? I fucking love her! We are having this baby, and we will be together. Mirela feels the same!'

Maureen was stunned, what the fuck was this kid going on about, she slapped Patti around the head, 'you are fucking 16 years old, you little knob head! You can't even look after yourself let alone a bleeding kiddie and a bird, and how the frigging hell have you been managing to knock about with a Pikey in the first place? How old is she? They don't let 'em off the bleeding site!'

Patti stood up, clearly in a state. He pointed a finger in Maureen's face as he yelled, 'don't fucking call her that, mam, I mean it. Mirela is my whole world and I won't have you slagging her off.' He lowered his arm and tried to compose himself, 'now, mam, are you gonna help us or not?'

Maureen could feel herself sobering up fast and it was far too nice a day for that. Thinking was for another day and right now she just wanted to have a good time. More than that, if Patti carried on raising his voice, all the punters would hear him and that would be a right showing up for her.

'Okay, son, calm down,' she said, standing up and patting her dress down, look, how far gone is the lass?'

Patti shrugged, 'we dunno for sure, but Mirela thinks it's about two months or thereabouts.'

Maureen raised an eyebrow and smirked, they'd obviously been at it for a while then, the mucky little gits. 'Right then,' she announced, smiling, 'we have some time at least before she starts showing. Time to come up with a plan. And I will, Patti, just give me a day or two to think of the best way to approach it, then we'll get together, me you and the lass, 'cos it's time I met her anyway, and we'll sort something out.' She was just about to leave Patti when she decided to give him a quick hug, 'get yourself off now, love, and don't worry. You're not the first and you won't be the last in a mess like this. But you're a King, son, you will deal with it.'

****

Patti was pacing the kitchen floor, smoking, as his sister poured him a glass of fizzy pop.

'Mum will go mental, Patti, if you don't open the back door, it stinks in here.'

'Oh, shut up, Dan,' Patti said, irritated by his sister's calmness, 'don't you think I've got bigger things to worry about than our mam having a go about smoking in the house?'

'Well, if you hadn't dipped your wick where you shouldn't have…' Dannielle raised her arms in submission as she saw Patti glaring at her, 'okay, okay, I'm sorry, but I'm with mum on this one, you should have taken precautions, Patti. And what's done is done isn't it, if you're keeping the baby, that's that.'

'Just fuck off, Dan,' Patti yelled, 'it's hardly as simple as that, is it? You only agree with our mam because she's got your lazy arse out of school, and letting you work on the frigging market. We still have fucking Bo Lee and the rest of the bastard psychos up there to contend with.'

Patti stubbed his cigarette out in the sink and stormed off to his bedroom. He should never have even told his stupid sister about the pregnancy and he certainly shouldn't have expected her to have his back after he'd told her what their mam had said. Not that he held out much hope for his mother stepping up either. No, he was in this on his own. It was down to him to sort it out.

The trouble was he had no idea how to do that.

If this had been some silly girl from the estate, it would have been different. Both families would have been there, having a piss up to celebrate, there would have been a bit of ribbing, but then that would have been it. His mam and dad would have gone all out to make sure the new baby had the best of everything, even before it was born, even his narky fucking grandmother would have got the knitting needles out.

It saddened Patti to acknowledge that because of the life Mirela had been born into, their baby would probably be an outcast. It made him even more determined to sort his situation out, but the surge of inexplicable love he suddenly felt, scared the shit out of him.

Chapter 17

Bo Lee was in Salford, Manchester, at an unauthorized traveler site, and he wasn't best pleased.

'You tell me now, boy,' he growled at Michael James as he held him by the throat, 'what it is you are insinuating about my daughter, before I throttle the fecking life out of you!'

'Please, Bo, let me down,' Michael begged as he fought for his breath, 'I only know what Chrissy has told me, please ask him.'

'Well Chrissy isn't here to ask, is he?' Bo yelled as he let Michael go, 'and it's you who passed comment about the trailer I'm here to buy.'

Bo Lee had travelled to Manchester to buy a two thousand pound trailer as a gift for Mirela. It would be stored elsewhere until her 16th birthday, and hopefully her wedding day, but it was a belter of a caravan and too good to miss.

Michael James had been going on and on about waiting till later and saying other bargains would come up, the whole of the journey, and now, as they strode across the muck, just as he was about to go see the bloke who was selling it, to pay him, the fucking gormless twin had spouted some shit about Mirela not being the daughter he thought she was, and the trailer not being worth the two grand. And now the little fecker was walking around in circles, shitting his pants about something.

'You best open your trap and speak, lad,' Bo Lee warned, 'because I'm buying this van for my daughter and Chrissy, and I'll not have you spoil the surprise, but if there's something I need to know, now would be the time because if I find out later on, that you've been hiding something, you will rue this day, boy, that I can promise you. You said Chrissy had said something to you, what was that?'

Bo hoped that his nephew hadn't been having second thoughts about taking Mirela as his wife. The Lee name depended on it, and if the lad had found himself another suitor it would be disastrous for Bo. There were no other suitable Lee boys who were still single, and besides that, he'd planned this big wedding since his daughter was a baby, even paid his brother, Brendan, a few grand years ago to seal the deal. No, his nephew wasn't getting out of this one, if that was his plan, he'd beat the living daylights out of him first. Fuck his brother tormenting him for the rest of his life about being unable to sire a gadje, and the Lee name ending with him.

'Chrissy was just rabbiting on one day, that's all, Bo, just saying that Mirela might fancy some other mush, like that Jimmy Jackson for instance, he's a fancy fella, all the gels swoon after that guy. He was just saying that the wedding wasn't sealed in blood is all, and I didn't want you wasting all this money for nothing.'

'Oh he did, did he, the fecking toe rag,' Bo raged, 'well I'll tell you this for nothing, boy, that fecking wedding *is* sealed in blood, or as good as, so you and that sackless nephew of mine best get your heads around it. If it's his wild oats he needs to sow, then he's plenty of time for all that.' Bo leaned in and stabbed a finger at Michael's head, 'I'm buying the trailer, shit for brains, so when we get back, you tell that Chrissy I best not hear any more shite about the wedding, you hear me?'

Michael nodded, 'it's a great trailer, Bo, and you're right, it's a bargain. You'll hear no more from me about anything. Your Chrissy was just probably having a case of the nerves, yeah, that'll be it, the nerves.' He smiled brightly, 'Leave it with me, I'll settle him down when we get back.'

Bo Lee's mother was said to have had 'the gift'. Not like old Bina, who told fortunes and bragged about her second sight, Ma Lee worked with her incredible intuition. As Bo sped up the M62 back towards Bradford, he was aware of an uncomfortable feeling swirling around in his belly. He remembered now how his mother would often speak of this, and how his father would base every single decision they made as a family on how Ma felt about it.

He remembered his mother clutching at her stomach and closing her eyes as she agonized about whether the family should move miles away, or if father should take a particular job or not. It was always the same, either Ma would smile and nod, or she would shake her head, and that was that. No arguments, she had the gift, and what she said was the be all and end all.

And she was always right, Bo thought as he glanced at Michael James nodding off in the seat beside him. Maybe Bo had the gift also? *Either that or I'm about to have the shits,* he thought, grinning at his own train of thought. He turned the radio up to quell his feeling of unease, and laid to rest all the doubts he'd been having about Chrissy's intentions towards his daughter. That trailer had been a proper touch and would set them up for life. Mirela would want it delivering to the same site she'd grown up on, and hopefully soon after the wedding, she'd have a belly full of legs and arms and Bo would finally get the little boy of his dreams. A grandson was just as good as a son any day of the week, life was definitely on the up. So why this fecking feeling that something bad was about to happen then?

Chapter 18

Chrissy Lee arrived at the West Bowling site around tea time, and headed straight for the twins' trailer. He knew Michael James had been off somewhere with Bo Lee, and he'd been on edge all day, hoping that his pal hadn't said anything about Mirela. Chrissy fancied the pants off the girl and knew she'd make a good wife. She already had all the tools of the trade for a traveler wife – she cooked, cleaned, looked after the babies, in fact the only thing wrong with her was her argumentative mouth. She fought against doing as she were told and that couldn't happen. She was still young though, plenty of time to get her in line and he had Bo Lee onside for that. The big fella always said his girl needed someone who could tame her.

The only other fly in the ointment was all the rumours about Mirela setting her sights on a gorger. Chrissy had been livid at first, but as time went by, and both he and Michael James had been keeping an eye on her, it seemed that the rumours had in fact been started by Mirela herself. No one he'd spoken to could say where they had stemmed from, and Mary Jane had laughed when he asked her. She told him that Mirela hadn't wanted to marry so young so she herself had started the whispers hoping that Chrissy would believe them and take his betrothal elsewhere. As he walked into the twin's trailer, he just hoped Michael James hadn't fucked things up by spouting off to Bo Lee.

'Tell me you haven't been running your trap to my uncle, Michael James, or so help me I'll swing for you,' he said, as he noticed his friend looked a little jumpy to see him, 'tell me you haven't?'

It was Mary Jane who answered first, 'sit yourself down, Chrissy, I've a beer in the sink for you, but listen, something *was* said today but you can't blame my brother, not a bit. He was trying to be helpful, so you'll hear him out. And before you blow a gasket, it was nothing bad, do you hear? Just listen!'

Chrissy groaned and held his head as his lifelong friend nervously explained what had led to him hinting to Bo Lee that there might not be a wedding, and that he'd tried to dissuade the man from buying a trailer for him.

'Oh, Michael, you silly bastard!' Chrissy yelled. He pointed his arm out towards Mary Jane, 'didn't you think to speak with your sister before you went? Eh? She knew! She knew it was all lies and gossip. My uncle will have my spleen for this!'

'But it's okay,' Michael James said, 'Bo was fine about it, and I swear to God, I never said we suspected anything, I just made out that Mirela might change her mind, her being so young and all, he was fine. He just said he'd have a quiet word with you, just to reassure you like, that his girl would be waiting for you and that you have nothing to worry about.'

Chrissy ran his hands through his hair. A quiet word from Bo Lee? There was no such thing. More likely it meant that the big fella would wall him up and half throttle him for even doubting his precious daughter!

'You should have said fuck all, Michael!' He hissed, 'that was the plan all along. Say nothing until we knew something, and we fucking didn't, 'cos there was nothing to know apart from the usual fucking gossip from the women.' Chrissy shook his head, 'I honestly think you spend way too much time with your sister, Michael, listening to the tittle tattle with the rest of them.'

Michael James shrugged his shoulders, 'I'm sorry, mush, I swear I am. Just blame me when Bo Lee has a word, tell him it was all gossip and that you never believed a word of it.'

Chrissy left the trailer practically quaking in his boots. He knew he'd have to go straight to his uncle and take it on the chin, whatever he had in mind. He was beginning to wish he'd never been betrothed to the silly cow in the first place, because now he knew he'd have to put up with Bo Lee for the rest of his life. Interfering in his business and watching over Princess fucking Mirela whenever he felt like it. There was only one way to deal with that, Chrissy thought as he trudged across the site, he'd have to frighten the girl to death, right from the get go, so she knew who her real boss was. Knock any thoughts of running to daddy right out of her head.

Bo Lee was sitting at a fire pit outside his trailer, cooking sausages, but he stood up when Chrissy approached.

'Now then, chavvie,' he greeted, kicking an upturned crate towards Chrissy, 'come on and have a sausage. Violet picked these up from the best butcher's in town today, take a seat.'

Chrissy cleared his throat and sat down, 'look, Bo, I don't know what that fucking divvy Michael James has been saying to you, but it's not his business and I can assure you here and now, there's nothing amiss as far as the wedding goes. He's been listening to shite from the girls and the gossips. Your little Mirela, well she's still a young 'un isn't she? You watch, she'll be as excited as I am by the time the wedding comes around.'

Bo Lee smiled and stabbed a sausage with a fork before handing it to Chrissy, he then looked him dead in the eyes, and still smiling, said, 'I don't give a bagful of fucks who's been talking shite, nor do I care what my daughter has been spouting about being too young for marriage. You will do exactly what's been expected of you since the day she was born. Anything else and you will lose an eye. Now, mush, do we understand each other?'

Chrissy was terrified, he had never seen such evil in a man, and the mad fucker was still smiling! 'We do, uncle, I won't let you down.'

'Well then,' Bo said, clapping his hands together, 'let's eat these fucking sausages, eh, lad?'

Chrissy left his uncle's trailer that night rethinking his plans about Mirela. The gobby little cow would simply have to be left to be gobby. He was under no illusions now about giving her a few slaps to scare her into being obedient. No, if he wanted to keep 20/20 vision, he'd have to leave her to it. Still, Chrissy thought as he stepped up the pace, towards his Landrover, it didn't matter a jot him taking Mirela as a wife. The mouthy mare could stay home all day and get on with her chores, while he continued to enjoy the life he'd become accustomed to, and that meant plenty of gorger gals for when he needed a bit of how's your father.

Chapter 19

Mirela lay in her bed, listening to the familiar sounds of night outside their trailer. Dogs barking, the odd fire crackling, cats wailing like babies. She thought for the first time, how comforting all of these noises were, and allowed herself to smile at the thought of city folk trying to sleep through it. That thought brought her mind sharply back to the present – to the real reason she barely slept anymore. She stroked a hand across her belly and could swear she felt a flutter. She mentally worked out that she must be around 10 weeks gone just now and she didn't know anything about pregnancy, other than it lasted around nine months and that sooner, rather than later, her slightly swollen tummy would become too big to hide beneath baggy clothes.

Mirela sighed and turned onto her side, glancing at her bedside clock. It was almost dawn, normally a time when she would simply give up the idea of sleeping and jump out of bed. But despite her lack of knowledge about impending motherhood, she did know that in order to keep healthy for her baby, she would have to get some sleep. She finally drifted off and into a dreamworld that was far more hectic than the comforting chaos of the site on which she had spent most of her life.

'I had terrible nightmares,' she told Patti, later that morning after she'd managed to sneak off to the scrapyard, 'I dreamed the women were all holding me down and the hag, Bina, was ripping the baby out of me, screaming it was the seed of the devil himself. It was awful, Patti.'

'That's just 'cos you're worried, babes,' Patti said, hugging her tightly, we all have nightmares when we're stressed, and you have a lot to be stressed about. I won't let anything happen to you, I promise.'

Mirela pulled back, tears spilling down her cheeks, 'but you can't promise that, Patti, how can you? Look at me! Soon everyone will see I'm to have a baby, and then what? They won't just disown me, Patti, they'll hunt you down and they'll hurt you, really hurt you. The dream was a bad omen, I just know it. My grannie had second sight, what if I have it too?'

What Mirela didn't tell Patti was that in her nightmare, her grannie, Ma Lee, had also been there, helping the women drag the baby from her, and she too had been screaming and cursing at her, but Ma had also warned Mirela that a darkness had been unleashed, and her baby would pay the price. Mirela shuddered as she remembered and was sure the dead were cursing her for daring to buck against tradition.

As much as Patti tried to understand their ways, he had no real way of knowing just how complicated life could get for a girl like her, who refused to fit the mould. She watched him, now, struggling for answers, yet she knew he had none that would help.

Patti stood up and started to pace in the tiny trailer, running his hands through his hair.

'I know you're scared, babes,' he finally said, 'and if you want the truth, I am too.'

He knelt down in front of her and gently took her hands, 'but, baby, I swear I will work this out for us. My mum knows, I told her, and if it comes to it, we can both live there. The baby too, she'll see to it that we have everything, Mirela, honest she will. Our Danni too, she'll help out and my dad, he'll come round, and he can definitely take care of us. Just say the word, baby, and we go there.'

Mirela threw her arms around this boy that she loved with all her heart. He absolutely didn't get it, she knew that, but she knew that he meant every word he said, and he really thought he could protect her.

'It's okay that your mum knows, Patti, I know you trust her, but we can't go there. I can't take the trouble to her door, and that's what'll happen. As soon as everyone finds out about you, then you and your whole family become targets. That's how they work. We can't do that, we need to get away, Patti, far away. We need money, and someone who'll help us.'

Patti sighed and stood up again, 'well we can have that too, baby,' he said. 'Mick will help us, I know he will.'

Mirela was puzzled, Mick Keenan? He had been a friend to her dad for years. Yes, he'd clearly kept his trap shut about her and Patti, but, surely he wasn't stupid enough to be a part of actually taking Bo Lee's only daughter away. It would be a death sentence for him.

'He would end up in his own car crusher, Patti, and you know it,' she said, 'it can't be him. He's already done too much for us.'

'No, you're wrong,' Patti said, his voice suddenly filled with excitement, 'there's stuff you don't know, Mirela, about Mick and your dad, but trust me, he *will* help us. He's the answer to our problems. He can get us away from here if we need it, and as for money; I can get my hands on that too! My dad has plenty and I'll find a way to get it. I just need a few more days, baby, but I promise you, I can do this.'

For the first time in weeks, Mirela felt a glimmer of hope. This wasn't Patti in one of his cocksure, I can do anything, moods, this was a side of him she hadn't seen before. It was as if he had transformed from boy to man in the space of minutes, and it gave her the feeling of being cloaked. The same kind of feeling she recalled having when around her father as a child. She allowed herself to smile as she stood up to hug him, and she welcomed that seed of hope to settle within her body, also cloaking the new life growing inside.

'I trust you, Patti,' she said, 'but it has to be soon, baby. The rumours about me are rife, and it's only a matter of time before I'm followed. I have to get back now, but I have someone too. Mary Jane, she's my friend and she knows everything. She will help us if I need her to.'

'Good,' Patti said, 'I'm glad you've got a friend back there, we need all we can get. Be safe though, Mirela, I mean it. I hate when you're back there and I don't know what's going on. Listen, get a bag together if you can, and hide it somewhere. Then if we have to go fast, you've got some stuff.'

'I will do,' she said before kissing Patti. A deep, desperate kiss that wouldn't lead anywhere, and only served to convince Mirela how much she loved and needed this man.

She got back to the site around lunchtime and after checking her dad's truck wasn't around, she headed for her mammy's trailer, keeping her eyes peeled for anyone who might be watching for her. The likes of Michael James and his little minions were flies in the ointment she really didn't need right now. As she opened the door to the home she'd always loved, she didn't notice the man she hadn't thought about in months. The man who had proclaimed his interest in her when she'd turned just 14. Jimmy Jackson watched sadly as she stepped inside the trailer and closed the door behind her.

Chapter 20

Violet Lee nudged her friend, almost knocking the china teacup from her hands, 'she's here, Della,' she said as the door opened and Mirela walked in, 'leave it to me.'

'Oh, hi, mammy, hi, Della,' Mirela said, smiling at them both, 'I think I'm going to have a lie down. I didn't get much sleep last night.'

'Oh no you don't, madam,' Violet said, standing up, 'you'll come on in here and sit with us for a bit. There's things we need to talk about.'

Violet watched the range of emotions flitting across her daughter's face and felt a heavy sense of dread. For days now she'd ignored the rumours flying around the site about her girl. It was par for the course living on a site within a small community. Tittle tattle was all it was, surely? Mirela wouldn't dare be sneaking off to spend time with a boy. A boy who wasn't her betrothed, and definitely not a gorger boy. She wasn't that stupid, was she? She certainly looked like a rabbit caught in the headlights right now.

'Don't look so scared chickadee,' Della said, causing Violet to scowl at her, 'it's just me and your mammy, we've been hearing some rumours is all.'

'I can tell by her face!' Violet spat, 'it's not all lies at all, is it, girl? What the hell is going on? I want the truth!'

'I don't know what you're talking about, Mammy,' Mirela said as she edged her way around the trailer to sit at the couch opposite the one Violet was at, 'what rumours? You know what the gossips are like around here.'

Violet felt like slapping her daughter, the cocky little mare. It was clear she was up to something, and she knew it now, it was written all over her face. She struggled to fight down the rage and remain composed as she stared at the girl. If all she'd heard was true, then Bo Lee was going to go ballistic. Minimum! Della had been with her all morning trying to get her to ignore the whispers, the knowing looks and the smug comments from the other women, but now Violet knew without a doubt it had all been justified. They all knew something she didn't. Well, she was damn sure she was going to get to the bottom of it.

'Just shut your mouth and listen, girl,' she said as evenly as she could, pointing a finger at her daughter, 'you've been sneaking off away from here and lying to me about it. That's a fact, so you can admit that first and foremost, right now.'

Mirela looked shocked and her cheeks reddened before she answered. 'Okay, mammy, you're right,' she said, 'I have been, but it's nothing sinister, I swear!'

'I fecking knew it!' Violet said, throwing her arms up above her head, 'and there's you, Della,' she went on, swinging around to her friend, 'there's you telling me I'm wrong, and that my *daughter* wouldn't be so stupid!' She turned back to Mirela, 'it's a boy isn't it? A fecking gorger at that!'

'Mammy, no!' Mirela yelled, 'no, it's not. I've been sneaking off to meet a friend is all, a girl I went to primary school with. I met up with her up at Keenan's yard with my daddy, she was there with hers and we got talking. I know I'm not meant to mix with her kind, I know that, but, mammy I've been so upset about the wedding and all, I just wanted to feel like a normal girl for once, that's all it is, I swear!'

Della stood up then and placed a hand on Violet's shoulder, 'Vi, at least it's not as bad as we were thinking. We knew the child was fretting about the wedding and who could blame her, hey? No harm can come from her meeting an old school friend now can it?'

'You keep out of it, Della Wright!' Violet screamed, 'you don't have a fecking husband like mine to explain it all to, because believe me, if we've heard about it, then so has he, and woe betide her once he's got all the proof he needs!'

'Mammy, please!' Mirela pleaded, 'please don't tell my daddy, and if he's heard the same rumours, just tell him it's all lies and that I've been here with you or Della, please, Mammy! You know I'm not like you, I need more than this…this site! What's so wrong in me having a friend? Danielle King is a good girl, she is, I swear, and I think her dad is friends with mine, she…'

'What did you say her name was?' Violet interrupted, 'and what's her dad's name?' She suddenly felt very sick and had to steady herself before sitting back down, 'it's not Pat King is it?'

Mirela nodded, 'Big Pat I think he calls himself. Do you know him too?'

Violet paled as her mind slipped back to the past and to the troubles her family had endured thanks to the King family. She prayed silently to god that her daughter wasn't going to bring them back into their lives. Composing herself as she noticed the odd look Della was giving her, she pointed at her daughter once more.

'I know them all,' she said quietly, 'and they are trouble, the fecking lot of them. Mirela, you listen to me now because I will not say this again. You stay away from that King girl from this very moment. You've had your bit of freedom and now it's time you became the woman you are meant to be. Your father is right. We've been too soft on you, and it stops now. You will marry Crissy Lee as soon as we can arrange it and you will accept you are one of us and that's that. You understand me, girl?'

Violet sat, helpless to do anything as her daughter burst into tears and ran to her bedroom, slamming the door so hard the whole trailer vibrated. Della opened her mouth to speak but Violet held up a hand to silence her.

'Don't,' she said, 'you have no idea about that family, Della,' she spat, 'and oh, sweet Jesus, if Bo Lee finds out who she's been mixing with, my life won't be worth living.'

'But why, Violet?' Della asked, softly, 'you're right, I don't understand. I mean yes, the girl shouldn't be messing around with the city folk, I get that, but she's at that age. I'm sure many other girls of our kind have had friends from the other side of the tracks. It's not the end of the world, and didn't she just say that Bo Lee is friends with the girl's father? That will make it easier on him, surely.'

Violet stared at Della. The woman hadn't been around back in the day. Way back before Mirela was born, and she didn't know the half of it. Only knew what she'd been told by the gossips about life before she'd moved onto the site, having travelled across from Ireland. Well, she wasn't going to fuel the fires any more than necessary. Della didn't need to know everything.

'Bo Lee has always blamed Pat King for the death of our first baby,' she said, knowing full well it was only a half truth, 'you'll have heard all about the accident with the horse, well it was Pat King who opened the gate that day. Anyway, it wasn't really all his fault, but the fact is, if he hadn't turned up when he did, our baby would have lived.' She sighed as she peered into her almost empty teacup to search for a sign in the leaves, 'so you see, Della, it's not just as simple as it seems. She can't be mixing with the Kings, Bo will fecking kill her.'

'Well, that's that then,' Della said, 'if that's the case, then Bo Lee can't find out. He loves that girl more than life itself, so we keep it from him. We make sure Mirela knows that she can't go off again and she can't see that girl, and we put the fecking gossips to bed. You threaten to go all Violent Lee on them if you have to, that'll shut them up.' Della laughed at her own joke, 'come on, Vi, it's been years since I saw you lose your head and swing those fists, let's put things straight.'

Violet allowed herself to smile at her younger friend. If only her husband could be so easy to persuade, but he wasn't. Bo Lee was nobody's fool and if he thought something was amiss, he would take his time to explore every angle until he got to the truth of it. He would go about his daily business as if all was well, smiling and joking, even with his sworn enemies, but inside he would be planning his next move. Becoming a gypsy king had taken years and there was no way he would be made a fool of, not even by his own daughter. Love her or not, if she wronged him, she would pay, just as anyone would.

'You're right, Della,' she said, 'we can sort this out, I'm sure we can. I'll get the twin, Mary Jane, to keep Mirela busy for a while. They seem close and the Gallagher girl can help prepare her for this fecking wedding, get her head out of her arse. Make her realise that our ways are our ways, and she can't fight against what's to come. But I swear by all that's holy, Della, the little mare best stay put from now on. If I hear she's been skipping off somewhere I'll kill her myself, so help me god.'

'She won't,' Della said, 'she's a good girl, Vi, she is. It's the thought of the wedding that's unsettling her, I'm sure of it. Our generation looked forward to it, it was a right of passage and we accepted it, but these days, with all the books and the schools and the mixing of cultures, well, it's no wonder the young girls believe there's more out there for them, and who can blame them, Vi, really? We never knew all the stuff they know, it's bound to be harder for her than it was for us.'

Violet knew her friend was right, but it didn't matter a jot. Their culture was as it always was and Mirela had to accept it. When Della stood up to leave, she hugged her.

'Go on, go and see to your little ones, my sensible friend,' she said, 'and don't worry, I'll do as you suggested – start a little bit of my own gossip to shut the nosey feckers up, and if that doesn't work then yes, Violent Lee might just resurface.'

Della laughed as she left the trailer and Violet stood in her doorway watching her walk off. She didn't react, but she saw Jimmy Jackson slinking back into the shadows of the trees round the side of her home. He was spying for Bo. That, she was certain of.

Chapter 21

Chrissy Lee helped himself to a bowl of stew from the stove in his friend's trailer, and grinned at Mary Jane, 'you're a good cook, twinnie, that's for sure. I hope you've been passing on tips to my wife-to-be. I know she spends a lot of time over here when me and Michael are off grafting.'

He watched carefully as Mary Jane busied herself at the sink, taking out the bowl for handwashing before replacing it with the dishes bowl and then ensuring the glass wear got washed up first. It was the done thing, and proved to Chrissy that this woman was good wife material.

In all honesty, if his father hadn't made the deal with Bo Lee all those years ago, he would have most likely pursued Mary Jane for himself. She was an alright looking gel – not stunning like Mirela, but good enough, and definitely a woman who knew her place.

Another big plus was that the twins had no meddling parents around. No interfering father to stick his nose into their business. The fatal car crash had been a tragedy when it had happened, the twins left to fend for themselves from the age of sixteen, but in Chrissy's opinion it had been a bit of a lucky touch. The brother and sister had never wanted for anything, ever. The men had given Michael James money every week, until he was strong enough to work and earn it, and the women had always taught Mary Jane how to cook, mend and get by.

'For a young girl, she's a very good cook actually,' Mary Jane said as she rinsed a glass, 'Violet has taught her well. She's great at cleaning too. To be honest, when she comes over here, we usually sew. She loves making nice things, she did the new covers for all my cushions.'

Chrissy rolled his eyes. Women stuff didn't interest him in the slightest and as long as he was fed and his sexual needs taken care of, that would do him. Even a mouthy, lairy little fucker like Mirela could be tamed or ignored. He turned to his best friend and mocked Mary Jane.

'Oh, take a look, Michael, at the fancy cushions, my home will be a little palace, what a lucky gadje I am!'

Michael James laughed and threw one of the rose gold cushions at Chrissy, 'it's `Mirela that's the lucky one, for sure, having a funny fecker like you to put up with for the rest of her life.'

Chrissy laughed along with his friend, but all the while he kept an eye on Mary Jane. He still wasn't convinced that the rumours didn't have a hint of truth in them, and if anyone knew anything, it was this girl. He couldn't remember if she'd always looked so on edge when he was around, but she definitely did today. Maybe she fancied him herself and she was a bit jealous about Mirela? Maybe that was it. After all, he was a good looking fella, plenty of the gorger women had told him that when they'd been after a roll in the sack with him.

'You alright, Mary Jane?' He asked, 'you've not heard anything else about Mirela and any fancy fellas have you? Only I happen to know that Bo Lee has a little spy following her about these days, so, if you're in on anything, you'd be in the firing line as well.'

Mary Jane finished rinsing the washing up before answering, 'you boys, and your bloody conspiracies, honestly! The poor girl is fifteen years of age, her freedom is about to be snatched away from her, forever, and this time next year she'll be expected to be thinking about having babies. How the hell do you think she feels? I can assure you both, chasing a bloody man around, gypsy or gorger, is the last thing on her mind. Just leave her be and let her get used to the idea. She'll be fine if you do that.'

Chrissy continued to study her for a moment before answering. He hadn't missed the reddening cheeks, so she clearly did fancy him. It was a pity she was his best mate's sister or he'd have definitely given her one, and maybe he still would if he got the opportunity. Just because a man got married didn't mean that the fish in the sea suddenly swam off.

'Alright, Mary Jane,' he laughed, 'calm yourself down, you can't blame me for wondering though, the girl's always round here according to Violet and Jimmy Jackson.'

'Jimmy Jackson?' Mary Jane asked, 'how the hell would he know anything? He's never round here if that's what you're insinuating. That fellow just fancies himself as a bloody Romeo, but trust me, he isn't as wanted as he would like to think.'

Michael James laughed, 'no, sister, he doesn't think that. Young Jimmy is keeping watch on Mirela for Bo Lee. He's been reporting back to all of us, but I think it's all good now. According to Jimmy the lass was sneaking off to meet a gorger pal she used to go to school with, he heard her and Violet screaming at each other yesterday in the trailer.'

'Is that right?' She asked, 'and which gorger might that have been? I mean, if she has, then she has, but it can only have been once or twice, like you said, she's always round here when she's not with her mammy or Della.'

Chrissy shrugged, 'some girl, who cares?' he said, 'let her go sneaking around with her little friends, it's no skin off my nose, she just better not get any townie ideas in her head, that's all. I'll put a stop to all of that soon enough anyway.' He threw another cushion, hitting Michael James on the back of the head, 'come on, mush, we need to hit the road if we're to be there before dawn.'

'You boys going out of town again?' Mary Jane asked as she collected the now empty stew bowls, 'you certainly make sure you have *your* freedom, even if us girls don't. Where you off?'

Michael grabbed his coat and the van keys, 'we sure do, sister,' he said, 'we're off to see a man about a dog down in Norwich, and the least you know, the better, capiche?

Mary Jane shook her head, 'a man about a dog indeed! Go on, the pair of you, get out of my trailer so I can clean up properly.'

Chrissy laughed. The more he got to know the better looking twin, the more he liked her. He decided to try give her a quick grope on the way out, without Michael seeing.

'We shall leave you to it then,' he said as he squeezed by her, ensuring he grabbed her arse during the manoeuvre, 'see you in a day or two.' He winked as the girl reddened again and scowled at him. She definitely fancied him.

The lads jumped in the Transit van and Chrissy started the engine. He slapped Michael on the thighs before screeching away on the gravel, 'she's a bit of alright, your sister, mate. If things were different…'

'Well, they're fucking not!' Michael James said, firmly, 'you can keep that dirty fucking trouser snake away from my sister, and I mean it, Chrissy.'

Chrissy laughed, 'behave, mush,' he said, 'as if I would, you're like family to me, I'd never!'

'Fuck off,' Michael said, 'Mirela *is* your fucking family, and you're definitely going there!'

They both laughed at that and then Chrissy decided to concentrate on the road. They had a long journey ahead of them, but it would be worth the mileage, Bo Lee had promised them that. Three grand to deliver a large parcel to a scrap dealer in Norwich. They knew what the parcel contained, it was special paper that was used for printing fake bank notes on. The dealer would hand over ten thousand pounds, three of which would go to Michael and Chrissy, the rest of course went to Bo Lee. All in all, life was good, and with Bo Lee soon to become Chrissy's father in law, it was set to get even better.

Chapter 22

Mick Keenan glanced around his desk at the various scraps of paper which served as his filing system. He opened the drawer and with his arm, scooped everything into it. Bo Lee had just pulled up in one of his pick up trucks, and it wouldn't do to have him or anyone else having access to the kind of information that Mick collated. For years, the scrapyard had served as a central information hub. Mick knew the kind of money that almost every criminal had access to, he knew the cars, vans and trucks that had had to disappear from the face of the earth, and he had hundreds of secret phone numbers.

 Names and details were coded in a way that was simple, but only known to Mick, but still, if someone such as Bo Lee wanted to find someone else, then Mick knew it wouldn't exactly take a genius to work things out. Just before Bo walked into the portacabin Mick slipped his hand into the small wire basket that had been fixed onto the side of the oak drawer. Re-assured that his gun was where it always was, he smiled to greet his long time associate.

'It's the gypsy king himself!' He said, grinning widely, 'what can I do for you, fella? Thought you had business down in Norwich this week.'

'How you doing, Mick?' Bo Lee answered, 'I decided to send the lads down yesterday, just the team of them. Not a big job like, nothing that would call for my presence. No, it's you I wanted to see.'

'No problem with those cement mixers I hope,' Mick said, feigning a worried expression, 'only I was assured they were top notch, lad, and you know the score around her, Bo, sold as seen.'

Bo Lee pulled a stool from the side of the room and sat opposite Mick at the desk. 'The mixers were grand, mush, it's nothing like that. It's about my daughter actually.'

Mick felt his arse cheeks clench as the gypsy's almost black eyes bore into his, but he continued to smile as he chose his words.

'Your daughter!' Mick laughed, 'I'm sorry, Bo, I know I've helped you with many things over the years, but I'm afraid I have to draw the line at babysitting.'

Bo Lee didn't laugh. He continued to stare, expressionless. Mick felt the hair on the back of his neck starting to prickle, and he knew the beads of sweat forming on his forehead would soon start to run down his fat face. *The gun's where it should be, and it's loaded,* he told himself in his head.

'You're serious?' He finally said, 'it's about your daughter? Has somebody hurt her, Bo? You need someone taking care of?'

'And you think I'd need you for that?' Bo finally said, a manic grin now spreading across his face, 'really? No, Mick,' he said, planting both of his huge hands firmly on top of the desk, 'what I need is answers, mush. The girl has been seen coming up here and I want to know here and now why that fucking might be.' He leaned across the desk then, almost nose to nose with Mick, 'and more than that, why the fuck you haven't said anything to me about that.'

Mick started to sweat more, and he knew that his fear must have been showing. In his youth he might have considered going up against a man like Bo Lee, but these days, with all the extra weight from years of fish and chip suppers four times a week, and a job spent sat on his backside most of the time, he knew he didn't have a cat in Hells' chance. He decided that brazen was the only way to go here. He shook his head and furrowed his brow.

'I swear on my dead mother's grave, Bo, I have no fucking idea what you're talking about, mate. Your daughter, up here? You mean without you?'

Mick flinched as Bo Lee thumped the desk hard, his huge hands now clenched into fists.

'Bo, I swear to you, I've only ever seen the lass with you, what are you talking about?'

'She's been followed here!' Bo Lee bellowed, 'seen, messing around with some townie lassie and a gadje. Who the fuck are they?'

He mentioned a girl first, Mick thought, maybe he could get out of this alive. He leapt straight onto the assumption.

'Hold your horses, Bo,' Mick said after a suitable amount of time looking puzzled, 'I might know what you're on about now then. But first, you should know, if your girl was up here, I didn't know it was her. When we had the fucking nonce ran out of town, I set Pat King's lad on working for me. As a favour like, the kid had left school and was getting into bother…'

Bo Lee banged the table again, 'get to the fucking point, Michael, or I swear I'll wring your fucking neck.'

'Like I was saying, he's the gadje you've heard of, and as for the girls, the lad has a sister who comes up here quite a bit. She drops him ciggies off or has messages from his dad. I seen her a couple of times with another girl, but they never come across here, so I'd have no idea who she was with. The lad always goes across the muck to see them. That must be it, Bo, that's all it was.'

Mick watched carefully as Bo Lee took in what he was hearing. He saw the struggle on his face as he tried to work out if Mick was telling the truth, and then he breathed a silent sigh of relief as the gypsy's black eyes softened.

'I mean, you can ask your man, Bo,' he said, 'whoever it was you had follow your girl, he will tell you, I'm sure, that I was nowhere near, so I couldn't have known if she's been up here.'

'I'll do just that,' Bo said as he stood up and placed the stool back against the wall. He turned to Mick and pointed, 'we've known each other a lot of years, Michael, you and I, and you know I expect the fucking truth in such matters. I'll be seeing you.'

Mick watched as Bo Lee strode off to his pick up, and realised he couldn't stand up. He really couldn't, his legs felt like they were made of jelly when he tried to. His hands were shaking too, but that didn't stop him from reaching for the small, loaded handgun from the hiding place, and stuffing it in his overalls pocket.

He would need to carry the gun now, everywhere he went, his life might depend upon it. He'd heard tales of men disappearing in Bradford over the years, rumours that their bones would never see the light of day, having been buried beneath tons of concrete at various housing development locations, and unfortunately Mick had played a part himself in the past when he'd been paid ridiculous sums to crush a car in the middle of the night, containing some dead body or other. Bo Lee's hands had orchestrated the deaths of almost every one of them.

His mouth suddenly felt very dry, so Mick reached back into his desk drawer and grabbed at the half bottle of Whisky. Ignoring the crystal cut glass tumbler – that was his celebration glass, for when a big job had gone well, he unscrewed the top and took a large gulp. As the amber liquid warmed his throat, Mick started to think straight, the gravity of the situation hitting him hard.

This was all going to come out. For getting involved with two stupid fucking kids, he could actually pay with his life. He needed a plan, and a fast one at that. A number of things needed to be done, and the first was to warn young Patti King. No point yet in getting Big Pat involved, that would start a war no one wanted, and it might not come to that if Mick was clever about it. Young Patti would have to do a runner with the girl, there was no getting away from that, and it had to be in a way that didn't involve Mick in any shape or form. The story would have to be that Mick knew nothing, and there couldn't be any evidence to say different. He really needed to know who the grass was, the one who'd told Bo Lee about Mirela being up there, and what exactly they knew.

Chapter 23

Patti rubbed his eyes and then squinted in the sunlight as he opened the door to see Mick Keenan standing on the steps. He'd spent the night on site, in the ramshackle caravan as Mick had asked him to take in some 'special' scrap that was being delivered in the early hours. For doing that, he'd been promised a lie in and a day off.

'Fuck's sake, Mick!' He said, 'what time is it? And why all the banging? Billy Arnold's stuff came in at about four o'clock this morning, I've only just shut me fucking eyes!'

'Never mind all that,' Mick said as he pushed by Patti inside the van, 'Jesus Christ, lad, it fucking stinks in here, you got a rat up your fucking arse, kid?'

Patti grinned, 'I had a Keema Curry last night, I'm afraid that chemical bog don't hide the stink of the shits, mate. I'll have it all cleaned away and smelling nice before Mirela gets here, don't worry.'

'Open them fucking windows!' Mick said before sitting on one of the bench seats opposite Patti's makeshift bed, 'then sit down, lad, I need to talk to you, and you're in shit street, mate, big time.'

Patti banged one of the windows open and then carefully carried the dirty chemical toilet outside. He could barely stand the smell himself and his stomach was definitely still dodgy from his late night supper. He could tell that Mick was getting frustrated and wondered what had gone wrong, because clearly something had, and it sounded like he was going to cop for it, whatever it was.

'Come on then,' he said, when he finally sat down, 'what am I meant to have done?'

Patti listened in horror as Mick told him about Bo Lee's visit and what had been said, but he almost shit himself when Mick pulled out a gun from his overalls.

'Fucking hell, Mick! What the fuck?'

'I don't think you understand what this means, lad,' Mick said, standing up and pacing, 'this is Bo bastard Lee. Not some numpty gyppo that's going to let it go. You're shagging his daughter! No, worse than that, you've got her up the fucking duff. What do you think happens next, eh?'

Patti still hadn't taken his eyes off the gun that Mick was now waving about as he spoke, 'but *that*, Mick, the gun, what you gonna do with that? We can't kill him!'

'I don't know!' Mick yelled, running his fat fingers through his hair as he paced the tiny van, 'I mean, he reckons he's got proof. Some fucking spy he's had following her. I mean obviously he won't know yet about the baby, he can't do, unless either of you have been blabbing. I should have just kept out of it from the start, what was I fucking thinking?'

Although Patti was scared now, he suddenly felt really sorry for Mick. The poor bloke, usually so laid back and not bothered about anything, looked like he was about to cry. Whatever had just happened between him and Bo Lee, the man had obviously kept his mouth shut about Mirela, and for that, he had Patti's respect.

'Neither of us have said anything about the baby,' Patti said, 'but it's not on you, Mick, I swear. No matter what happens now, I will never drop you in it. You knew nothing, and that's that. This is all on me, I will swear down that we were going behind your back. I mean, we could be alright, yeah? You said he looked like he believed you about our Danni. He might just leave it now.'

Even as he said it, Patti knew it was bull shit. From everything he knew about Bo Lee, he was certain that the man wouldn't just leave it. It was bad enough if he thought Mirela had been sneaking off to meet up with a townie girl, she'd be in big bother for that in any event, but if he had an inkling she was running off to meet some lad, a lad that wasn't Chrissy fucking Lee, her life wouldn't be worth living. Either way, there was no way he was going to get involved with murdering her father.

'Mick, I'll think of something,' he said, 'but I'm not going to tell you what we're doing. That way, you can't be accused of getting involved, but please, mate, put that fucking gun away, there's no need for that, that's just asking for trouble.'

'Patti, you're going to have to leave here, mate, you know that, right? I mean, it isn't safe for you for a start, and it won't be safe for me if I keep you on now that Bo Lee's on the war path. I'll make it right with your dad, I'll tell him the police have been sniffing around so I'm laying low for a bit and there's no work for you. I'll give you a couple of hundred quid, lad, to get you started, but you're going to have to go, and if you're with Mirela, you'll have to leave Bradford, kid, you know that.'

Patti's arse cheeks clenched, but this time it wasn't anything to do with the Ruby Murray he'd gorged on the night before. This is what real fear felt like. He ran to the van door just in time to puke his guts up.

'I'll be alright,' he spluttered as he wiped a hand across his mouth, 'I'll get my stuff and leave here, Mick, I know what you're saying, and thanks for all you've done for us. I swear down I won't drop you in it, no matter what happens.'

Mick nodded and made his way outside, 'I'm sorry about all of this, kid,' he said, 'young 'uns like the pair of you deserve to be left to choose who you like. All that pikey shite is old fashioned. They need to join the real fucking world, but it is what it is, and there's fuck all we can do about it. Here.' He shoved a roll of cash into Patti's hand, 'it's just what I had in the office but it should sort you out for a bit. Don't stay round here though, lad, get yourself off for a few months. Forever if you're taking that lass of yours with you.'

Patti watched, sadly, as Mick trudged back up the yard to his portacabin. He stuffed the notes into the pocket of his jeans before going back inside to think. Suddenly it seemed time had ran out. No more making plans that never materialized, no more promises of someday soon.

That someday was upon them now. The problem now was that there was no way he could go back to the gypsy site now that Bo Lee was on the warpath. He would have to pack up what he needed, go back home and then try somehow to get word to Mirela. He had a feeling that she'd have no idea yet about what her dad knew.

Chapter 24

Danielle was searching her stall in John Street Market for a pair of American Tan tights. Her customer was a right miserable bleeder and was getting on her nerves.

'What size did you say? Large?' She asked the woman, who was 'tutting' impatiently.

'44 hips!' The customer snapped, 'I get them here all the frigging time. Where's Pauline? She knows where everything is. You're bleeding useless!'

Danni took a deep breath before noticing her brother was sniggering at the corner of the stall. 'Here,' she said, 'American Tan, size 44, and in future don't be so bleeding ignorant or I won't be serving you.'

The woman snatched her tights and slammed her money down on the counter top. 'Frigging kids! No wonder this country's going to the dogs!'

'I'm impressed, sister,' Patti said, laughing as joined Danielle, 'how do you manage to keep your cool with people like that? At home you're a right gobby mare.'

Danielle laughed, 'trust me, it takes every ounce of patience I can muster. Anyway, what you doing here? Mam sent you for some new knickers?'

'Oh, give over,' Patti said, pulling a face, 'can you imagine that!'

Danni noticed the pained look on her brother's face. Something was wrong. He had never come to see her at work before. She checked her watch, 'Pauline will be back from her dinner in five minutes, Patti, why don't you nip round to the Wimpy and get us a table. We'll get burgers and milkshakes and have a catch up. My treat, it's payday.'

'Bloody hell,' Patti said, grinning, 'what's the world coming to when my little sister offers to buy the scran? That woman was right, Dan, it's going to the dogs.'

She watched as her brother sauntered off out of the market and then checked her watch again. Pauline was her boss, and although she expected meticulous timekeeping from her staff, she was always late back from her own breaks. Not that Danni ever complained, she was grateful for the job and it beat going into school everyday. All she had to do was keep her eye out for the truant officer and all would be well.

John Street Market was a great place to work, Danni loved it and spent all her wages in there. It was a large undercover market with stalls and shops from which you could buy anything – make up, underwear, clothes, pots and pans, toys, ornaments, anything you could think of, you could get in John Street, but it was the hustle and bustle and the regular characters that Danni loved best.

There was old Anna, some called her Polish Anna, others said she was Russian. Whatever she was, it was certain she had been a prisoner of the second world war and had been experimented on. The gossips said that the German's had injected her with all sorts and tried to turn her into a man. She would scream and shout all around the market but all the stall holders either loved her, or were afraid of her. They would see to it that she was given free food and drinks, but all gave her a very wide berth.

A good thing too as Anna always carried a walking stick – for some reason this had loads of baby's dummies hanging from it, but if groups of kids started to torment her, as they often did, she would lunge at them with her stick and give them a good beating if they weren't fast enough to run off. She'd then laugh her head off at an alarming volume and start singing at the top of her voice.

The other regular character was only known to Danielle as the one legged match man. He stood by the entrance to the market, in on old brown suit, with a tray of matches strapped around his neck. He was quiet and kept himself to himself, but he got lots of customers for his match books, and even those who didn't require them would feel sorry for his one leg and chuck coins onto his tray. And then there was 'Jesus'. No one seemed to know his real name, but the rumours were that he had never aged in years. He simply wandered around the market – the whole of the town centre in fact, smiling at everyone he passed, bare feet and wearing only a long, brown robe. It was said that when he smiled at you, he gave you good luck, so Danni always made sure she caught his eye.

Spotting Pauline making her way back to the stall, Danni grabbed her purse from under the counter and her cardigan from the hook on the wall. 'Is it okay if I go for my dinner now, Pau?' She said, 'only our Patti has come to meet me and we're off for a Wimpy.'

Pauline pulled a face, 'rather you than me,' she said, 'bloody American shite it is, but go on, take an hour love, it's quiet today, I can manage for a bit.'

It had just started to rain, but the Wimpy was only four doors down from the market so Danni hitched her cardigan over her head to protect her new, bob hairstyle, and ran quickly to meet her brother.

'Can't believe it's pissing it down,' she huffed as she joined him at a table and picked up a menu. 'I bet I look a right bleeding state now!'

'Don't bother with that,' Patti said, 'I already ordered us both a Wimpy brunch – I know you like those, and since you offered to pay, we got Brown Derby's for afters. And, Dan, you don't look any more of a state than you usually do, so stop flapping.'

'Cheeky Pillock!' Danni said, laughing, 'and it's a good job I've still got last week's wages left then isn't it? Dinner and pudding! Anyway, I've got a full hour today, so you're honoured. Now, what's up, 'cos it's obvious something is, or you wouldn't be here.'

She watched as her brother seemed to struggle with what to say, and wondered what on earth was wrong. It wasn't like him to be lost for words and it made her feel uncomfortable.

'It's about me and Mirela,' he finally said, 'I mean, you already know that she's pregnant, and yeah, that's bad enough. Thing is, sis, chances are that her dad's going to find out. He's apparently had a spy watching her. Some gyppo off the site, he's been following her. Bo Lee came up threatening Mick Keenan this morning, Mick never told him anything but still, he knows something and he's trying to find out who I am.'

Danielle's jaw dropped as she stared at him, 'you serious?' she asked, 'oh my god, Patti, you're dead, the both of you! What are you going to do? She's definitely keeping the baby then?'

She suddenly felt really sorry for her big brother as she watched him wringing his hands together and hanging his head, he looked afraid, and this made Danni afraid. 'What you gonna do, Patti?' She asked again, gently, as she reached to place her hand on his, 'is Mirela planning on keeping it? Because if she is…'

The food was delivered to the table at that point, but Danielle had lost her appetite.

'Yes, she's keeping the baby, course she is! None of them up there know she's pregnant, not yet, and they don't know about me for definite,' Patti replied as he picked up his knife and fork, 'and she's not showing yet, not really, so we got some time to plan, but until then, I need your help, sis. I've had hell on this morning. Mick's had to sack me, he daren't keep me on anymore, I can't get no messages to Mirela in case I'm seen. She will most likely go looking for me up at Mick's and when he tells her what's happened, she'll freak out and not know where to find me, I need your help!'

Danni was confused, 'my help? What on earth can I do about any of this?'

She listened as her brother explained his plan, which was as mad as it was simple. According to him, Bo Lee was almost believing the story that Mirela had in fact been meeting up with Danielle, and it was only accidental that Patti had sometimes been there. In order to make it more convincing, Patti now wanted her to be seen up at the site, asking for Mirela, and to also make an appearance up at Keenan's yard.

'And how am I meant to do that, you div? I work full time for a start!'

'You'll have to throw a sickie or something,' Patti said, 'I don't know, but I need you to do this, Danni, or we're fucked! We already need to make plans to fuck off out of Braford, but this would just give us a bit more time to get sorted out first.'

The thought of losing her brother for good upset Danni a lot. They'd always been close, it was only recently, since Mirela had been in the picture, that they'd drifted apart, and it made her feel angry. But despite the chasm developing between them, Danielle really hoped it wouldn't come to him having to leave town. Life with her parents was already unbearable, but without Patti there, it would be absolute shit.

'I can't believe this, Patti,' she said, shoving her plate away, 'if Mirela cared about you as much as you say, she'd get rid of that baby to save your arse! If you end up together forever anyway, there's plenty of time to have more kids.'

'Stop it, Dan!' Patti spat, 'don't you see? Even if there was no baby, we'd be together somehow, so we'd still have to move away to do that. She's meant to be marrying her cousin for fuck's sake! But there is a baby, and we're keeping it, we want it, and that's that. Now, are you going to help us or not?'

Back at work, Danielle didn't have to work too hard to convince Pauline that she was ill, her boss noticed the change in her the minute she got back from her break.

'You're coming down with something, kiddo,' Pauline said, feeling Danni's forehead with her hand, 'a bit of a temperature as well. Get yourself off home, lovey, and go to bed. Get your mam to give me ring in the morning if you're still badly and I'll get Carol in to cover for you.'

'If you're sure,' Danni said, miserably, hardly believing she'd agreed to her dumb arse brother's request, 'only I feel shocking, Pau, I think it might be the flu or something.'

Ten minutes later, Danielle was upstairs on the bus, on her way to the traveler site. Lighting up a cigarette as she stared out of the window, she had a feeling that she was about to enter into something that she should definitely turn away from. It was too late now though, Patti was her brother and he needed her.

Chapter 25

Violet Lee was on a mission. Mirela hadn't left her room again all morning and it looked like she was set on spending the afternoon in her pit as well. She knew the girl was pretending to be asleep every time she looked in on her, punishing her for daring to tell her that she'd best do as she were told. Well, no more. It was about time Violet showed her daughter, and everybody else, who called the shots around here. Pulling on her short boots and grabbing her cardigan, she set off, marching across the site, glaring at anyone she crossed paths with. First stop was the Callaghan twins.

'Jesus, Mary and Joseph!' Mary Jane exclaimed as she answered the door to Violet's banging. 'Oh, I'm sorry, Violet, I didn't know it was you.' Her tone had changed to apologetic, and she lowered her eyes, 'If you're looking for Mirela, she's not here yet.'

Violet looked Mary Jane right in the eyes, she prided herself on reading folk, and if this girl knew anything, she was about to get it out of her.

'My daughter is safe and sound in the trailer, thank you,' Violet said as she walked past the girl and went on inside, 'it's you I wanted to see.'

'Cup of tea?' Mary Jane asked as she reached into a cupboard for her China.

Violet pulled a face. As if she would take a cup of tea from a young gel who had no husband, and no parents helping her out. Who knew what dirt and grime could be lurking. 'No, thank you,' she said, noting the girl's blushes, 'could you just sit for a minute, please, I want to talk to you about my Mirela.'

As Mary Jane settled herself on the grey, velvet sofa, Violet took in the trailer. If she was being completely honest, she was impressed by the cleanliness. It was quite pretty too. Not expensive or filled with treasures like her own van, but nice, clean lace curtains and a few polished brasses adorning the walls. The pale pink cushions looked good too, edged in a rose gold rope, clearly the girl had some pride in her home, maybe she could have accepted a cup of tea, she mused.

'What's wrong, Violet?' Mary Jane asked, sounding slightly nervous, 'only I've heard the rumours about your girl running around with some city folks and I wouldn't believe the half of it. In fact, and I know this to be true, it was Mirela who started off the gossips herself.'

'What are you talking about?' Violet snapped, 'why on earth would she start off tittle tattle about herself? And what do you mean, city folk? According to Mirela it's just the one lassie she's been off with.'

Violet listened as Mary Jane told her all about how Mirela thought she was too young to marry, and how she was afraid of Chrissy Lee, and then how she came up with the idea of spreading rumours that she had met some boy, in the hope of the Lee boy believing her to be soiled and calling the wedding off.

'She knows it was silly of her,' Mary Jane went on, 'and she promised me it was all lies, and I believe her, Violet. I mean, she's here practically every day, and if not here, she's running errands for Della or the other women. She told me about the girl she used to go to school with, said she'd met her a couple of times, but I swear to you, that's all I know.'

'Well, she wasn't here with you yesterday or the day before, I know *that*,' Violet said, 'and she wasn't with Della either, because Della was with me. So, what's she doing when she's not here? I expect you, as a full grown fecking woman to put the girl straight.
It's alright for you, Mary Jane, you own this trailer, you have your brother earning for you. My daughter needs a husband and Bo Lee expects it.' Violet stood up and pointed at the girl, 'you know more than you're letting on, I'm not stupid. Where has she been going?

'I've just told you everything. The only other place I've known her to go recently was last week when she went to see old Bina,' Mary Jane said, her voice cracking, 'and she posts letters for everyone down at the shops, but I swear, Mrs Lee, that's all I know.'

Mrs Lee? It was Violet up till now. The girl was terrified for sure, and Violet knew there must be a reason for it.

'Fecking Bina?' she said, 'why in God's great name would she be going there? She hates the woman, all the children do! Come on, gel, spit it out because I know you know more than you're letting on.'

Violet was shocked to see the girl burst into tears. What the hell was going on to have her so shook?

'Can you please leave me, Violet, please. I promise I can't help you, and I just don't want trouble at my door. All I've ever done is love and look after your Mirela, ever since she was tiny, you need to speak to her.'

As Violet strode off, she realised she was shaking. Heading towards Bina's old trailer, she had a feeling of doom settling upon her and she knew that the answers she sought, when they came, would only serve to make matters worse.

'I wondered when you'd show your face at my door,' the old hag cackled as she opened her door, 'been many a year, Violet. I suppose you should come inside.'

'If I had any choice I wouldn't fecking be here,' Violet snapped, careful to not touch anything as she stepped into the dingy, stinking van. 'And watch your fecking tongue with me, Bina, because I'm not afraid of you, or your fecking curses, I was cursed by your mouth years ago so you can't scare me now. I want to know why my daughter has darkened your doorstep, and nothing else. I'm not interested in your babble.'

Bina laughed loudly, the crackle from her lungs making her sound like a fairy story witch, and reached for her pipe. Lighting it and inhaling deeply, she then reached onto the side of the kitchen sink and picked up a tarot card. Throwing it on the floor in front of Violet, she grinned as the woman bent to pick it up with her hand shaking. It was the Tower. A bad omen indeed, a sign of major shock out of the blue that would completely destroy lives.

'She came for a reading,' Bina said, 'but didn't stay to hear it all. That was her third card and I put it aside for this day. See, I knew you'd come here seeking the truth, and I want you to have it. The cards are never wrong, Violet, it's how we read them that matters, and I've known for years what's to become of you, now sit, stand or whatever, but you will listen.'

By the time Violet left the old hag's trailer, she was in a blind panic. She couldn't process what she had heard and knew that even when she did, she didn't know what to do about it. But do something she must. She didn't see the girl until she'd banged into her and almost knocked her over.

'I'm so sorry,' she said, realising straight away that this girl wasn't one of their own, 'I'm in a world of my own today. Can I help you? You looking for someone?'

'It's okay, I'm fine,' the girl said as she straightened up her clothing, 'I was looking for Mirela Lee, she's my friend, do you know where she lives?'

Violet stared hard at the girl, her heart sinking. The prophecy that Bina had just spoken about was starting to come true before her very eyes. She suddenly knew exactly who this girl was. The same eyes, the same hair as her slut of a mother. The same woman she'd fought with years before, a lifetime ago.

Back when she, like her own daughter, had thought she could escape the life she had been dealt, that she could have escaped with the first man she had fallen in love with – a secret she would take to the grave, but old Ma Lee had put paid to that. She'd made her realise that there was no escape. That she'd been born into the life, and to avoid being shunned she must let go of all fanciful thoughts and marry Bo Lee.

'Well now,' Violet said, folding her arms and pursing her lips, 'you must be the very same gorger that my Mirela has been running around with. Danielle King is it?'

The girl was jutting her chin out as she replied, 'It is. And it's very nice to meet you, Mrs Lee. Would it be alright if I go see her for a little while? I've just finished work and I promised I'd see her this week.'

Violet stared, open mouthed, she couldn't believe the girl's cheek. Like it was all okay to be wandering around up here on the site, like she wouldn't be in kind of danger, the little fool. Had it been any later in the day the girl would have encountered the dogs for a start, or the lads coming back from their grafting, and then she'd have been in trouble. She wouldn't be so cocky if she knew what she could have walked into.

'No, it's not alright, and neither are you it seems, not right in the head,' she finally said, 'and that daughter of mine must have been touched by your stupidity, girl. In fact, my Mirela is in a whole load of trouble for mixing with you and your kind. You need to leave here right now, and I don't want to see you up here again, do you hear me?'

'Why?' Danielle asked, 'I'm not causing any trouble, we used to be in school together, we're friends.' Again, she stuck her chin out, 'I actually think it's awful how you treat her and keep her up here like a prisoner. Can't I just see her for five minutes? Check she's okay?'

Violet couldn't believe her cheek, the cocky little mare, but then again, this was Maureen King's daughter, so she was bound to be as bold as brass. 'I said no, now go on, feck off,' she shouted, struggling to keep calm, 'and tell the rest of 'em the same. If I see you up here again, I'll set the fecking dogs on you. One word from me and they'll have your guts, girl, now *move* it!'

The girl looked like she might say something else but then thought better of it and turned to walk slowly away. Violet watched her till she was out of sight and then walked slowly back to her own trailer. What Bina had said had blown her mind to pieces, shattered any fanciful thoughts of a happy ever after for either her daughter or herself, and she needed to think. For now, though, she had to pull herself together because neither Mirela nor her husband could know what she knew. Not yet.

Chapter 26

Mirela was shaking from head to foot. She let go of the curtain and sat down heavily on the sofa. It was Danni that her mother had been talking with, of that she was certain, and she had sent her on her way. What the hell was going on? She couldn't ask her mother, who was now on her way back, or it would rouse suspicion and another argument, but there had to be a good reason for Danielle to dare risk coming up to the site, and all Mirela's instincts were telling her that something was seriously wrong. She felt a surge of panic as she imagined it might be Patti in trouble. If her dad had done something to him, it didn't bear thinking about. She suddenly felt ill for real.

'Oh, you're out of your bed then?' Her mammy asked as she came through the door, 'feeling better are you?' Her tone was strange; sarcastic and flat.

Mirela tried to avoid meeting her mother's eyes, but she knew that she was being watched intently, she had to get out of here somehow, and she needed to be clever about it.

'I still feel badly, mammy,' she said, running a hand across her forehead, 'I got up for some water, but I keep going hot and cold.' Mirela bit her lip and risked checking her mother's expression as she went on, 'do you think I could take a walk to the chemist to get some paracetamol, mammy? I really think I need it, and the fresh air might do me good.' She knew very well that neither of her parents kept medications in their van, it was just something they never did.

She watched as Violet turned her back and started to rattle around in the china cupboard for her favourite cup and saucer. After setting it down she turned back around, smiling, and said, 'you get yourself comfy, girl, I'll not have you traipsing around for your own medicine when you're not well. I'll make you a nice cup of tea and then I'll go to the chemist for you.'

Mirela's heart sank for a moment, but she quickly realised that this was still an opportunity to escape. If she moved fast, she could get dressed and sneak away while her mother was gone. She smiled at the woman who had spent her life tending to the needs of her family – disregarding her own, and felt a pang of guilt that she would soon have to hurt her in a way that would no doubt destroy her. She had a sudden urge to hug her tightly but she couldn't.

'Thank you, mammy,' she said, 'I do love you, you know, you're so good to me. I know I give you and Della headache when I go on about stuff, and I'm sorry, mammy, I swear I am.'

'It's alright, my girl,' her mother said, busying herself again with the tea making, 'I'll just make you this and I'll go for the paracetamol. You rest, chicken, and stop it with the soppy talk, it makes you weak and you need to be getting strong just now, not wasting away in your bed.'

Mirela took the cup and saucer when it was ready and sipped her tea, watching her mother prepare for a trip into the next village where the chemist was. It was only a fifteen minute walk, but her mammy, like all of the other gypsy women on site, would always get changed out of their every day clothes for the occasion, and brush their hair into a tidy style. Their 'city' clothes, as they called them, would be given a good wash when they returned, but were necessary so that the women blended in with the other shoppers, the gorgers, who would otherwise stare at them, and whisper behind their backs.

Some of the younger women delighted in the fear they caused, and would often speak in loud dialect and pretend to put a curse on the poor city girls. Mirela's mammy never did that though, but she would snap if she thought she was being talked about and would give anyone who wronged her a mouthful.

Mirela frowned and put her teacup down as she continued to watch. This was new. Her mammy had been back into the big bedroom after changing her outfit to a floral dress and a lightweight, belted, beige coat, and was now wearing a pink lipstick and some blush on her cheeks. Mirela couldn't remember ever seeing her mother wearing make-up. Her hair, usually straggly and hanging down, was now scoped up into a bun on top of her head, held in place with a pretty pink flower pin.

'Wow! Mammy,' she said, her eyes widening, 'you look beautiful! But you're only going to the chemist, I've never seen you so done up. Best not let Daddy see you like that, or you'll have him getting jealous.'

'Hush, child,' her mammy said, a faint blush deepening the already rosy cheeks, 'for your information I've got more than your medicine to worry about. I need the butcher and the post office as well, and I might get the bus into town yet too. Have a walk, clear my head. Will you be alright on your own? I don't want you going out till you're well, do you hear me?'

Mirela nodded, too stunned to speak. She'd never noticed how beautiful her mother was before. Before she had the chance to say anything else, her mammy picked up her handbag – the one she only ever used for weddings or funerals, and left. Mirela couldn't see her mother's tears as she made her way through the site.

She gave it ten agonizing minutes before leaping into action. Something was wrong, she could feel it in her bones, and she knew she had to find Patti to find out what it was. She also had an awful feeling that when she left the van this day, she wouldn't be able to come back. With this in mind, she walked into her little bedroom, reached into her wardrobe for the bag she had once carried her books in, back when she went to school, and started to stuff it with what she deemed necessary.

Underwear, two baggy summer dresses, three loose fitting tops and two pairs of elasticated waist shorts. The only jeans that still fit her, she had on. Not a lot of belongings for the rest of her life, Mirela acknowledged sadly, but it would have to do.

The next thing she did made her feel guilty, but again, she knew it was necessary. She walked into her parent's bedroom and felt under the left side of the mattress, the side where her dad slept, and lifted it up. As she expected it was stuffed with money. Notes of every denomination, and lots of them. It looked in disarray, but Mirela knew her dad would have counted every penny, and would know exactly how much had been stolen, but still, she grabbed a handful and stuffed these into the bag with her clothes. Finally stepping outside into the early Autumn sunshine, she sighed heavily. The scrapyard would have to be her first port of call.

Mirela almost jumped out of her skin when Mick Keenan flung open the door of his portacabin before she had the chance to knock. She was even more stunned when he reached out and grabbed her roughly by the arm.

'What the fuck are you doing here?' He hissed, pulling her inside after wildly looking up and down the yard, 'Jesus Christ! If anyone's followed you!'

'Followed me here?' Mirela said, the feeling of dread she had, intensifying, 'what do you mean, and where's Patti? I need him, urgently.'

Mick shook his head, sadly, 'Patti won't be back, love, I've had to lay him off. Sit down a minute, 'cos you obviously have no idea what's going on, but then you have to go. You can't be seen up here, sweetheart. If your dad turns up, my life is over.'

Mirela burst into tears as she listened to Mick. For all of Patti's promises, he hadn't been able to sort anything out at all. Now they'd have no money and nowhere to go, and she definitely couldn't go home now, because according to Mick, her dad knew everything.

'Does my dad… does he know about the baby?' Mirela asked as she sobbed, 'and who the hell has told him all of this?'

'He doesn't know you're pregnant as far as I know,' Mick said, 'in fact I'm sure he doesn't or he'd be tearing the town up by now, but I've found out that it's a young 'un called Jimmy Jackson who's been spying and reporting your whereabouts. Snidey little bastard he is, he'll have it coming to him, don't you worry about that.'

Mirela couldn't believe it. Jimmy Jackson. The lad she had fancied since she was about eleven years old, was there no one she could trust? She knew she had to put those thoughts to one side for now though, for now she had to make a plan.

'I don't have much time, Mick,' she said, and pointed to her bag, 'I've taken what I need, and I can't go back. I won't go back, but I need to find Patti, fast. My mother will be back there in a couple of hours and I need to be far away by then, before she gets them all searching for me.'

Mick leaned forward and gently took one of Mirela's hands, 'are you sure you have to do this, love? I mean, they won't let you carry on seeing Patti, and your dad might never speak to you again, but I know your mammy, love, and I know for a fact she will come around and support you and that baby, even if it means that you and her are shunned, but at least you'll have her. I know Patti loves you, but he's a young boy, how's he going to look after you?'

Mirela knew that Mick was afraid for her, and he had every reason to be. She knew he was only trying to help, but he didn't understand, not really. She loved Patti and that was that. She would be with him and there were no other options as far as she was concerned. She took a tissue from her pocket and wiped her eyes before blowing her nose.

'You've been a good friend to us, Mick,' she said, smiling, 'thank you for everything, but could you please give me Patti's address so I can go see him. Please, Mick.'

Ten minutes later, after a glass of milk and more time convincing Mick, Mirela had the King family's address and was on her way. Mick Keenan had told her it was a half hour walk and given her the straightforward directions, so she was confident she knew where she was going.

Chapter 27

Maureen King was tipsy. Both kids were out somewhere, and she had the house to herself. Her mates, Kate and Elaine had both knocked her back when she'd asked them if they were up for a session at the pub, so she'd been to the off license and bought a couple of bottles of wine. Having already sank one bottle, she was now dancing around her living room, hairbrush in place of a microphone and watching herself in the mantle mirror as she danced and sang along with the radio.

'I got you to hold my hand, I got you to understa-a-a-and, I got youuuuu babe!' She was having an air guitar moment when she heard the banging on the front door.

'What the fuck!' She cried when she saw who it was – a woman she wouldn't forget in a hurry even though it had been years ago when they'd had a fist fight about Mick frigging Keenan of all people! 'Violent Lee as I live and breathe. What the fuck do you want?'

Violet scowled and stared straight at Maureen, 'you need to invite me over your threshold, Mrs King,' she spat, 'what I have to say isn't for the ears of your neighbours, unless of course you want them all knowing about your dirty little secrets.'

Cheeky cow! Maureen thought as she stepped aside and checked up and down the street. She didn't want any of these nosey bleeders telling big Pat she'd had a frigging gyppo at her home, especially this one. 'Come on in then,' she said, theatrically, 'don't let me stop you.'

Maureen watched as Violet took off her beige coat and folded it neatly across her arm. Her mind was racing. What did this woman want with her after all these years? Her alcohol fuddled mind suddenly fell on the answer. She had somehow found out about her and Bo lee. It had to be that. They had spent a weekend together years ago. Drugs, sex and booze had been all it was, but Maureen had known the man was married, and so was she. It hadn't stopped them though.

'Listen, Violet, I think I know why you're here,' she said, wondering if there was to be another fist fight, 'but let me tell you now, it isn't what you think.'

She watched the confusion flitter across the gypsy woman's face, but decided to go on. She had to make this out to be someone else's fault, and she was good at that.

'There was no love involved, no feelings, I can promise you that. In fact, it was practically rape, and I take no pleasure in telling you that, and I'm truly sorry about it, but you need to know the truth.'

* * *

Jimmy Jackson had heard enough. He moved away from the letterbox and left the neat front garden, closing the gate quietly behind him. He felt sick for Mirela but now at least he knew the truth, and as soon as his truck could get him back to the site, so would Bo Lee. The man's daughter hadn't gone astray at all, far from it. The poor girl had been raped and now Jimmy knew exactly who had done it. He made some calculations in his head as he drove through the estate.

This had been going on for some time, so if she'd been raped, surely she wouldn't have continued seeing the mush? Was he forcing her? He could have been threatening to tell her dad of course, that would have been enough to frighten Mirela into carrying it on. That must be it, Jimmy told himself, blackmail. The Mirela he knew was an innocent, but now she would be seen as damaged goods. Chrissy Lee wouldn't want her now, or would he? Jimmy knew how callous the Lee boy was, and if he went ahead with the wedding, he would forever treat her like a dog, that was a certainty, and Bo Lee wouldn't step in, not if Chrissy had been so good as to marry the girl with such a reputation. Whatever the outcome, it wasn't going to be good for Mirela, Jimmy thought sadly, half wishing he'd never agreed to be Bo Lee's spy.

* * *

'Fecking shut your cake hole, you stupid bint!' Violet snarled as Maureen continued to bleat about her misfortune years earlier. 'Do you think for one sorry moment I care that you and my husband rolled around in the fecking hay years ago?' She threw her hands up in the air, 'for feck's sake it was a blessing that there were little tarts like you around. It kept his filthy paws away from me.'

Maureen was confused and fell silent. It wasn't about that? Well, she'd just stupidly landed herself in it for nothing then.

'Oh,' she said, 'well why are you here? I don't understand.'

She watched as Violet once again straightened her coat across her arm, patted it and then sat on the edge of the nearest armchair. Maureen sat on the sofa, sobering up by the minute.

'Why, Violet?' She asked again.

'I need a glass of water,' Violet replied, her voice trembling, 'we have to talk, Maureen, but I'm not sure where to start.'

Maureen brought a glass of water and sat back down, wondering what on earth was so important that it had brought this woman to her home. She had a sense of foreboding and suddenly felt very sick, and as she listened in horror while Violet spoke and she knew she was in some kind of nightmare.

She heard the words, but her brain couldn't make sense of them. Violet was telling her that the girl her stupid son had got pregnant was this woman's daughter. Bo Lee's daughter. This couldn't be right, it couldn't possibly be right. She had to stop her talking.

Chapter 28

Mirela's heart leapt as she turned onto Quaker Lane to get onto Canterbury Estate. Right there, walking towards her was a familiar figure. It was Patti, she started to run to him. 'Oh my god, oh my god, Patti, I've been so scared!' She cried as he pulled her into his arms. 'Everyone knows about us, everyone! What are we going to do?'

'Mirela, thank god,' Patti said, kissing her head, "I sent our Danni up to see you, to get a message to you about what happened at Keenan's, did she tell you?'

'She came up,' Mirela said, 'but she bumped into my mammy and she wouldn't let her near me. I knew something was wrong though, so I sneaked away, I went to Mick's and he filled me in. But Patti,' she pulled away and looked into his eyes, 'I feel so bad.

My mammy was so nice to me, it was like she was coming round to my side or something, I don't know. All I know is that I had to find you. I've brough money with me, and my stuff, I can't go back, we have to go away. Today. Like now.'

Patti took the bag from Mirela and looked inside it and sighed, 'we'll be loaded for a bit then, babes,' he said, 'Mick Keenan gave me a few hundred quid, and I've robbed my dad's stash, but Mirela, there's not a lot of clothes in here. If we're going, we can't come back, you're going to need more.'

'We can buy more,' Mirela said, allowing herself to smile for the first time that day, 'I mean, this belly will start to get bigger by the day, so I'm going to need bigger things.' Suddenly feeling more confident than she'd felt in weeks, she put her arms around his waist, 'but you'll need some stuff too, Patti, will you be able to get some? And where will we go? Oh my god, Patti, I'm actually excited. I mean I'm terrified too, but I'm excited.'

Patti laughed, 'the world is our oyster, kiddo!' He shouted at the top of his voice, picking Mirela up and spinning her around.

'Put me down, Patti,' she giggled, 'think of the poor baby, it'll come out dizzy!'

'With my genes, babes, it'll come out dizzy anyway,' Patti joked. "come on,' he said, grabbing her hand, 'our Danielle is at her mates and my mum's getting up close and personal with a few bottles of the vino. Let's go for a walk, give her half an hour to pass out, then we'll sneak in, nick a few of our Dan's outfits for you, and get my stuff. We can go to the park and plan where we're going to go.'

Mirela couldn't help smiling as she and Patti lay side by side on the grass under a huge oak tree. She knew she was in a very dangerous situation, and that by now probably the whole site were out looking for her, but right now, this felt so right. If only she could capture this moment in time and then live in it forever, she would be forever happy. This is all she had ever wanted, to be with a boy she loved, without a care in the world and to live happily ever after.

Her mammy might say that it was only in fairy stories that such things happened, but Mirela was going to be the exception to the rule, she was going to take this happiness no matter what she had to lose to have it. She remembered once reading a Jackie annual, one that a friend at primary school had bought from a jumble sale and kindly given to her. She got to the Cathy and Claire problem page and had been stunned to learn all the ways in which you could tell that a boy liked you.

One of them had been that if your hands accidentally brushed together and the boy then held on to it, that was a sure sign. She smiled happily as she noted that she and Patti were laid here, hand in hand.

'I have an Auntie in Kent,' Patti said, breaking her thoughts, 'I've never met her, but she's my dad's sister and they write to each other, so I could easily get her address, we could go there and find her. She would put us up for now and keep quiet about it, I know she would because her and my dad were really close when they were younger.'

Mirela shook her head, 'she's family, Patti, and it's family we have to stay away from. I mean she might be lovely, and I don't mean anything by it, but it's my daddy. As soon as he finds out what I've done, he will stop at nothing to get me back. So, if your family are involved, no matter how far away, we would be putting them in danger. We need to go somewhere to start afresh, where nobody knows us.'

Patti nodded thoughtfully, Mirela was right, the less his mam and dad knew the better. Just like Keenan, if Bo Lee came calling, they would be genuinely in the dark.

'It'll have to be a boarding house then, I reckon,' he said, 'a bed and breakfast at the seaside or something. We look too young to go looking at renting a house, and we *are* too young I think, but those places, those B & Bs, they don't care who you are so long as you're paying up front. We've enough money between us. We could pay for like two weeks in advance, then I could get a job before any more is due, that way we've enough to get all the things we need for the baby.'

Mirela felt a surge of love and leaned in to kiss her gorgeous boyfriend, 'see, this is the Patti I need right now. The one who has the answers and knows exactly what to do. I love you, Patti King.'

'And I love you too, Mirela Lee, soon to be King,' Patti said, 'as soon as we can, babes, we're getting married.' He stroked her stomach, 'this baby will have two married parents, I promise you.'

Music to Mirela's ears. She could see it now. Her and Patti returning to Bradford in a car that Patti owned, a wedding ring on her finger, a beautiful baby strapped into the back seat, girl or boy, she didn't really care, and a gorgeous, satin trimmed Silvercross pram in the boot. Eyebrows might raise, but nobody would dare to call her a failure, and if she was still shunned, who cared? Not her, she would have everything she had ever wanted. She was disturbed from her daydreaming as Patti pulled her arm.

'Come on, kiddo,' he said softly, 'let's get going. Mum will be snoring in her bed by now and you and me, we've got a train to Blackpool to catch.'

Blackpool, that sounded perfect, a place where everyone went for their holidays, a place filled with fairgrounds, happiness and endless beaches. The pair of them held hands tightly as they walked back through the estate up to Patti's house. Mirela had never been so excited in her life, and they were just a few hours away from freedom. 'You sure your mammy will be asleep, Patti?' She asked as they neared the house.

'Course she will,' he said, 'she can't take her alcohol that woman, but it doesn't matter if she isn't. She knows about you and knows we're keeping the baby. I'll just tell her we're off away for a couple of days, she won't say anything, she won't care. My dad's working away so as far as she's concerned the fewer people she has to worry about the better.'

As Patti pushed on the front door, he held a finger to his lips, 'shush, no point waking her if she's comatose,' he whispered, 'come on, I'll just leave her a note.'

Mirela followed Patti in, but then wondered why he had suddenly stopped in the entrance, leaving her unable to move any further. Pushing lightly on the small of his back, so she could see what the problem was, she stepped inside and then also stopped suddenly, trying to make sense of the scene before her. The woman staring at her from in front of the fireplace was obviously Maureen King, Patti's mum, but sitting in the armchair in front of the window was her own mother.

'Mammy?' Mirela half whispered, 'what's going on? please, let me explain.'

She was beyond shocked when her mammy leaned her head into her hands and began to wail uncontrollably. She glanced at Mrs King, but she too was now crying. Silently, but tears streaming down her face causing thick, black lines to appear down her cheeks from her mascara. Someone had to have died, that was it, there was no other explanation for this, none.

'What the fuck is going on here?' Patti yelled, regaining his composure, ''cos if this is about splitting us up, you've no chance. None of you. We're together and that's that, and if you don't like it you can all fuck off, because we're off us. We'll just fuck off somewhere and you'll never see either of us again. Or the baby.' He turned to the armchair by the window, 'because yes, she's pregnant and it's mine, and we're keeping it. We love each other.'

Violet Lee started to wail even louder and began rocking in her chair, pulling at her own hair. Mirela was terrified, and it suddenly occurred to her that whoever must have died, must be someone close to home.

'Is it my daddy?' she screamed, 'is he hurt? Has something happened?'

Mirela ran to the back of the room, where Patti was now standing, and fell to her knees. 'Oh please, god,' she cried, 'please let it not be him. Please!'

Chapter 29

Bo Lee was like a raving lunatic. Wild and irrational at the best of times, what he had just been told had sent him way over the edge. Jimmy Jackson had being watching and listening out for him and had now told him everything, so he knew without a shadow of a doubt what he must do. The fucking King boy! Big Pat King's lad, of all people! This was going to cause a war, but the lad had raped his only daughter and now he was going to pay. He threw his sawn off shot gun into the Land rover and forced himself to take some deep breaths.

'You sure you don't want me to come with you, Bo Lee?' Jimmy Jackson asked at the window, I could follow in my truck and then if you need me to bring Mirela back while you sort things out, I can do.'

Bo shook his head, 'no, son. You can't be seen anywhere near the place. What I have to do needs to be done by my hand alone, the police will come. You can't be there.'

Jimmy glanced at the gun and asked nervously, 'you're just going to scare them, right? I mean, they're only kids aren't they? The lad deserves a good hiding though, and… and scaring to death, yeah?'

'Go on, Jimmy,' Bo Lee said as he revved his vehicle, 'you've done well, lad, go home and forget all about it, you hear? Not a word to anybody else.'

Bo watched through his rearview mirror as the sneaky Jimmy Jackson sloped off trough the site and then did a wheel spin in the dirt as he set himself to task. That fucking little cunt, Patti King, was going to die today, and Bo wouldn't feel one pang of guilt about it. That family had cursed his for almost 20 years and it would end today.

If Pat King came after him, so be it, though in Bo Lee's mind, the man should leave it. The bible says an eye for an eye, and that's what this was. A son for a son. All those years ago, if Pat King hadn't chosen that day to come up to do his dirty dealing, Bo would have had the son he craved.

Mirela might still have been born, but his first would have been a strapping boy, one who would carry on the Lee name. Instead, he was having to practically force his daughter to marry a cousin so that could happen. All down to the fucking Kings.

As his Land rover screeched to a halt outside the house he barely remembered any more, he didn't notice the neighbours out in their gardens watching nervously as events unfolded. It wouldn't have mattered though, everyone knew this place kept business to themselves. It wasn't like any one of them would even think of interfering, or worse, calling the cops, not yet anyway.

Bo Lee didn't bother to hide his gun, he simply reached across to grab it and then jumped out of the driver seat, swinging it manically from his arm. He knew Pat King was working away, which was a shame. He'd have liked to have dealt with them all at once, but these matters couldn't wait. Pat could get his comeuppance another time.

'Open the door, slag!' He bellowed as he banged on the knocker, 'I know you're in there, and so is my fucking wife. Open up or I swear I'll kick the fucking door in.'

Maureen King answered the door and Bo almost knocked her to the floor as he stormed in, to be met not only by his wife, but also his daughter and the scumbag King lad. He raised his gun and as his face contorted, he pointed it towards the boy, 'it's fucking you I'm here for, boy' he snarled, 'but then you'll know that, won't you? Now that my fucking wife is here.' He glared at Violet but never moved his gun away from its target. 'And you, woman, to think you knew this was who our daughter was running around with!'

Patti looked terrified as he answered, 'all this because I love your daughter, I don't understand. What is it we've done that's so wrong?'

Violet stood up, 'put the fecking gun down, Bo, right now before you do something you'll live to regret. The kids have only just got here, they don't know what's going on and neither do you, are you listening to me?'

'Oh, I know enough, woman, trust me, and this little bastard is going to pay.'

Maureen then tried, 'Bo, there's something you should know. I know you think you know what's going on, but we all need to sit down, calmly, and talk.'

'Mam!' Patti yelled, 'what the fuck? What is it? Look at Mirela, she's traumatized! Why's he here with that gun?'

Bo Lee looked at his daughter then. This lad had raped her, what the fuck was he on about, love? And why was she clinging to him like that?

'You fucking raped her!' Bo Lee screamed, still aiming his gun, 'my fucking little girl, and you raped her, you filthy scum!'

'No, Bo!' Violet yelled, 'He did not! You don't know the half of it, we're all fecking cursed, oh drop the fecking gun, Bo, and please listen.'

Bo Lee scowled at his lying wife. She's just been told the story not twenty minutes ago by the slag standing by her side. Jimmy Jackson had heard every word, the boy had raped her. That's exactly what Maureen King had admitted and he wasn't listening to this shit any more.

'On your fucking knees, boy,' he shouted, 'and get the fuck away from my daughter!' He cocked his gun and aimed again.

Mirela screamed, a piercing scream that seem to travel all around the room. 'No! Daddy, I'm pregnant! I'm having Patti's baby, your grandchild! Please stop, Daddy.'

Bo almost faltered, he couldn't take in what was being said to him and he felt confused. A baby? Mirela was pregnant? What kind of monster took an innocent girl, a betrothed, innocent girl, and raped her, leaving her with child. This was all wrong, the boy had to die.

He pulled the trigger, too late to see Mirela lunge in front of Patti King and take the shot that removed half of her face.

Patti King roared as he threw himself at Bo and began punching and kicking at him. Bo fell to his knees, unaware of the screaming women, slithering around on the blood covered floor, trying to tend to Mirela, or the blows that Patti was raining down on him. He simply stared at his daughter's half head. He suddenly realized the enormity of what he'd done, and he threw Patti, still screaming, to the floor and began to choke him. The boy, with his blood splattered face, swelling with the pressure, tried desperately to pull Bo's huge hands from around his neck.

'No!' Maureen screamed, yanking at Bo's hair, 'no! Let him go. Please, Bo, please don't kill him. He's your fucking son!'

Suddenly there was silence. Mirela was clearly already dead, the women weren't speaking, and after he let go of Patti King's throat, the boy seemed stunned too. Bo Lee began to wail like a wounded animal and he looked to his wife for some comfort, but there was none. Violet, looking like she'd been savaged, simply nodded to confirm what Maureen had said.

His son? His mind leapt back to the past as he slowly turned to look at the lad he hated, and he knew at once it was true. A reflection of his own younger face was staring back at him. That gorger bitch had bore his son and kept it a secret all these years. It hit him then, the child his daughter was carrying, his fucking grandchild, would have been born of incest. He hadn't known she was pregnant, he hadn't known any of this. As his mind splintered, he began to rock. He gave no resistance when the police arrived to take him, and he looked at no one apart from his dead daughter.

Chapter 30

Violet Lee felt as if she were living in a dream. A nightmare from which there was no waking up, and all of her actions were simply automatic. Relatives and friends from generations back had turned up at the site the night before to offer their condolences and to attend the wake of her beloved daughter. Thankfully, the council and other authorities hadn't turned up to turf off the steady stream of trailers that had arrived throughout the day and parked up, illegally, all the way down the lane near to the site.

All day and night, groups of people had been in and out of her van, blessing Mirela and willing her to rest in peace – always careful to keep their distance for fear of getting contaminated by death. This was a strange death indeed for a Romany child, with so many conflicting elements.

On the one hand, the death of a child was always more traumatic for the grieving community, and the wailing and lamenting for a young life lost, could be heard constantly until after a funeral had taken place. On the other hand however, in this case, the child had died in sin, carrying the unborn baby of a city boy, and who would have been surely shunned if she had lived.

This left the mourners with quite a dilemma – did they bless the dead girl, despite all her sins, and wish her peace, or did they risk the wrath of her spirit returning as a Mulo, and bestowing vengeance upon them? Violet guessed they all went for the former – afraid for their own salvation and long lives. She couldn't care less either way, as her own life was now forever ruined. Her daughter gone – her only child, and her hatred for her husband was palpable. As if reading her thoughts, Della came to sit with her.

'Won't be long now, Violet,' she said, 'I've had word the cars and carriages are making their way up the lane. Are you going to be okay?'

Violet stared at her friend and knew that Della was the only one she could really speak to.

'I hope he fecking rots in there, Dell,' she said, rocking slightly as tears ran down her face, 'I hope he loses his fecking mind and lives there in torment for the rest of his days.'

Della squeezed her tightly, 'I've heard he's getting fifteen years, Vi, and he'll serve every one of them in torment, don't you worry about that. It's you I'm worried about, my friend, and what's to become of you after this day is over. You know you have me, right?'

Violet nodded, fighting the urge to throw herself down on the floor and scream till she had no breath left. She wanted to die, she wanted to rip her own insides out, and most of all, she wanted to scrub the image of her daughter's dead, mangled body from her mind. She had only looked into the casket once, and was so desperately sad that her beautiful Mirela's face had been carefully covered with a black, lace veil. The mortician had asked Violet to choose a favourite outfit to dress her in, and now her tiny body looked lost in the white blouse and skirt she'd worn on her 15th birthday. The baby had been removed – still born, from her womb, and disposed of. That had never been spoken about by anyone since, and Violet still couldn't bring herself to think about it. A boy, the hospital had said, well so fecking what!

She nodded at her best friend, 'I thank God every day for you, Della,' she said, 'and for everything you've done to help me through this. I just want this day over.'

Violet stood up abruptly and took a deep breath, 'right then, I'm ready,' she said, 'will you hold me, Della, as we walk through?'

'Of course, I will,' Della said, standing and linking arms with Violet, 'and remember, Vi, you don't have to speak to any of them, do you hear me? This day is about you. And Mirela. Anyone dares to speak of Bo Lee and you fecking spit at their feet.'

The funeral director and his men took the signal and lifted up Mirela's coffin, to make her final journey to the cemetery. Violet had insisted on this, refusing to allow Chrissy Lee and his father to be any part of it. The two women followed behind them, walking slowly in between the two rows of wailing mourners that now lined the route through the site to where the black cars were parked, waiting, and then made their way to the front, to climb into the beautiful, Shire horse drawn carriage. Both burst into tears again as they watched the casket being carefully placed into the glass booth at the back.

****

Patti King was devastated. How was this day even possible? Only days ago, he'd been the happiest he'd ever been in his life. He and Mirela were all set to go off to Blackpool and start their lives together. He just couldn't get his head around it, and he couldn't make any sense of the fact that he'd found out that Mirela had been his sister. How was *that* possible? They were in love, having a baby, surely all those feelings would have felt wrong, and they didn't. Even now, now that he knew, he couldn't accept it. That that animal, Bo Lee was his biological father.

That his dad, Big Pat, was in fact his step dad, and Danielle his half sister. It was all too much to process. He felt as if he'd cried a million tears for his loss, but didn't know how he would get through this day. Could he cry at the funeral? They all knew. The gypsies that didn't want them there would be watching, and they'd curse him if he cried, because in their opinion, Mirela was never his to have.

'You look lovely, son,' his mam said, smiling at him as she walked into his bedroom, 'very smart, you'll do her proud.'

'Don't, mam,' Patti said, 'I know you think I'm some kind of sicko, like that lot up there do, so don't try be nice to me.'

Maureen sat on the edge of his bed, looking sad, 'Patti, please, baby, don't be like that. None of us knew, if you'd told me her name in the beginning I would have told you, I swear I would have, none of this is your fault.'

Patti spun around, fuming, 'no! It's fucking yours!' He yelled, tears spilling once again, 'if you weren't such a slag, none of this would have happened.'

'Oi!' His dad shouted, appearing in the doorway with Danni, 'I won't have you speaking to her like that, lad. I don't give two fucks what you think, me and your mam have made our peace with it. It was a long time ago, and no matter what, I'm your dad, so just leave it out with the accusations.'

Patti snorted. Made their peace with it? The house had been a battle zone for the past week, with his dad calling his mam a lot worse than a fucking slag. What he meant was, that as usual, his mother had won. Had somehow turned everything around so that his dad felt it had been his fault all those years ago, for neglecting his wife and concentrating on building his business. He'd even heard him fucking apologizing to her! He was about to say as much when he noticed how upset Danielle looked, so instead, he took a deep breath before speaking.

'Sorry dad,' he said, 'I'm just having a hard time with all of this. Let's just get through today, eh? You gonna be alright, Danni? I promise you, sis, you don't have to come, I won't mind. It's not going to be nice because none of them want us there, we can only hang about near to the grave.'

Before Danni could answer, Big Pat sneered, 'and who gives a fuck what that lot think, lad? Any of those cunts dare try stop us and they'll be burying a few more today, that I can promise you. Your sister will be fine, we all go as a family and that's that.'

****

Violet could barely breathe. This was so unlike any other funeral she had ever attended. Normally the procession would consist of the coffin, the cars and 100s on foot, all slowly going by all the places that meant something to the deceased – pubs, places of work, places they would regularly visit, but in Mirela's short life, she had been nowhere, done nothing. Was it fair that the Roma children were kept like prisoners and not allowed to live a life outside? Had Della been right all along? It was too late now though, and the only place they had diverted to had been her junior school. Then straight to the church for a service which only proved, yet again, how little Mirela had lived, and now, now she was about to be lowered into the dirt. Forever gone.

The wailing grew louder, the women dropping to their knees in sorrow, and Bina started her regular chanting as the men hung their heads in reverence. Amid the noise, Violet, still held tightly by Della, looked to the skies, unable to bear the sight of her daughter disappearing from view. Her spirit was free now and she would be heaven bound to sit with the angels and wait for her mammy. For the first time in days, violet smiled as she imagined Mirela's journey to the everlasting, but as she lowered her head so say her final goodbye, that was when she saw him.

She held her breath as she locked eyes with Patti King. The boy who had stolen her daughter's heart, the boy who was the seed of her husband. She expected to feel repulsion, and was surprised when she didn't. He continued to stare right back at her as she realized that what she felt was pity. He was a victim too. Violet felt a sudden surge of something within herself and tried to put a name to it, but she couldn't. All she knew was that her life wasn't over after all, she still had a purpose. At the end of the service, and to the gasps of everyone present, Violet made her way across the plot of land, to where the King family were standing alone, all dressed in black. She ignored Bina's yells about the Devil's seed, and her curses, and finally stood in front of Patti, who had never taken his eyes off her.

'Thank you for coming,' she said, simply, 'Mirela would have appreciated it.' She leaned in closer then as she added, 'and I'm sorry for your loss, boy.'

She felt the presence of her daughter and it took her breath away as Patti put his hand on her arm and replied 'she will always be with us, and thank you, for this.'

Violet looked at the whole family before speaking again, and then back to Patti, 'I hope you will come see me, when the dust settles, Patti, and talk to me about the last few months of Mirela's life. I need it, son, is that okay?'

She then turned away and walked back to the confused onlookers. She marched across to Della, linked her arm and pulled her towards to gates. 'We'll walk back, Del,' she said, 'give them something to fecking gossip about.'

Chapter 31

It was the middle of January, and Patti was starving and freezing. He'd just finished a ten hour shift up at the scrapyard and had come home to a plate of warmed up fish and chips for his tea.

'You know I hate 'em like this, mam,' He yelled, 'they go all soggy and shit, how many times do I have to tell you?'

Maureen shrugged, 'well I'm sorry, your highness, but until you start paying me the same board money as your dad does, I won't be cooking you fancy bleeding meals, and stop gobbing off at me or you'll get a smack round the bleeding chops!'

'Don't worry, ma, it won't be for much longer,' Patti replied, grinning, 'I'm 18 now, and as soon as I get across to Sheffield and pick up my new trailer, I'll be off, so you won't have to worry about cooking me anything. That suit you?'

'You can piss right off!' His mam yelled back, 'it's bad enough your frigging sister has pissed off with her simpleton of a bloke, I'm not losing any more money!'

It had been a year and four months since Patti had lost the love of his life and it had changed everything about him. No longer was he a scrawny 16 year old without a job, he was now practically running Mick Keenan's yard, and as his dad had said more than once, he was built like a brick shit house. Mick had taken ill after a stroke a year ago, and had insisted that he only trusted Patti to run his business. Patti had been happy to step in, it gave him something other than grieving to do, and he soon learned the ins and outs of the trade. Mainly the illegal trade which he had now expanded so that it was taking ten times the money it had when Mick had been sorting it. The cars were still the mainstay, but when Patti had introduced forged notes and drugs into the mix, Mick had had to have a room cleared out at his home to house the safes.

'And why the bleeding hell would you want to live in a trailer, up at the yard, when you've got a lovely home here? Maureen continued ranting, causing Patti to laugh at her.

'It's not just a trailer, mam,' he said, 'it's a fucking mansion of a trailer, costing me six grand and that's half of what it's worth, but I doubt you'll ever get to see it, mother, because it's not getting sited up at the yard. Why would I want to live up there when I work there half my life?'

Maureen stopped buttering bread and stared hard at Patti, 'so…so if you're not living up there, where then?'

Patti shook his head and sighed. His mother never listened to a word he said. For months he'd been telling her about how well he was getting along with Violet Lee, and how she had learned to love him and felt like part of her daughter lived within him. For months his mother had ignored him when he chatted about how he was making a name for himself up on the site, giving jobs to the gypsies when it was required and sorting out trouble for them if it was needed.

Because Patti was a natural fighter it had turned out, and the rage that was always bubbling away inside of him meant that he was an animal in a battle, and it had served him well. He was respected and feared by the gypsies who had learned to accept that Violet needed him, and the fitter and bigger he became, the more they revered him.

'You know where, mam,' he said gently, watching as she struggled to contain her emotions. Patti wasn't stupid, he knew that the couple of hundred quid a week was the great loss, but he also knew that his mam would be afraid of breaking the news to his dad. For all of Big Pat's promises, he had never been the same man after he'd found out that Patti was Bo Lee's illegitimate son, and had spent even more time working away from home. 'Look,' he said, standing to put an arm around her shoulders, 'I'll still see you right for money, mam. I wouldn't just piss off and leave you without, would I?'

Maureen gazed lovingly into his eyes, 'what, you mean like 200 a week, son, same as always? Aw you're a good lad, Patti, a lot better than our Dannielle, the tight little mare she is. Him a bleeding drug dealer an' all, and never gives me a bleeding penny!'

Patti laughed, clearly his sympathy was misguided and he was right the first time. He was just another wage packet and so long as she wasn't going to lose it, she couldn't give a toss where he lived.

'There you go, ma, all happy again,' he said, 'now, fuck these soggy fish and chips. How about I jump in the car and go pick us up an Indian with all the trimmings. A couple of bottles of wine as well, to celebrate, eh?'

'Oh, that'd be lovely, son,' she said, 'and get me a couple of them onion bhaji's too, I love them, I do.'

As Patti queued for his meal, he reflected on recent events. It had been Della Wright's daughter, Daisy, who had put him onto the trailer in Sheffield. One of her cousins had acquired it and needed it off their site, fast. A base had then been cleared for him at West Bowling and now all he needed was a work free day to go and collect it. He had become close to both Violet and Della and they treat him like their own family. It had been a shock to him at first, after the funeral, to find how powerful the urge had been to be up there, where Mirela had spent all of her young life, but he had soon realized that 'up there' was the only place on earth where he could be himself. A place where he felt no guilt about his relationship with the girl who had been his half sister, and where the community had vowed never to speak of it. They had accepted him because Violet had, and that was good enough for him.

Chrissy Lee had moved away of course. As soon as the funeral was over he'd taken himself off, miles away, to start afresh and find himself some other wife, but Patti had never forgotten what he'd done to Mirela, and his name was etched just as deeply as Bo Lee's on his mind's revenge list. His thoughts were broken as the young girl behind the counter started speaking to him.

'I've put you extra chapattis' in, Patti,' she said, smiling shyly, 'and they've made your Keema just as you like it, extra hot.'

Patti grinned, he was used to this kind of attention from the local girls, they all thought they were in with a chance.

'It's Patrick these days, love,' he said, winking at the assistant, 'but thank you, I'm sure my mam will appreciate it.'

As he walked back to the car, he wondered what had made him say that. Patrick King? Patrick King Junior? He grinned to himself and looked up into the night sky, *you're right, baby,* he thought, *a name much more suited to a man. Time to leave the boy behind.*

Chapter 32

Daisy Wright watched with interest as the four men worked on installing the massive new trailer. From her mammy's steps she had the perfect vantage point, and it made her giggle as she listened to them swearing and shouting out to one another as they tried to get it all level. The trailer itself was a beauty, the size of which Daisy had never seen before, and she imagined what it must be like inside. Nothing like the trailer she'd lived in all her life that was for sure, her, her mammy and daddy and brothers and sisters all squashed up into two little bedrooms and a sitting room that became their parent's bedroom on a night.

She sighed as she imagined what a luxury it must be to not have to dance around with your legs crossed when you needed a wee and there were two or three others waiting for the bathroom before you. At almost years of age, she knew it was high time she found herself a man so that she could marry and have a trailer of her own. She sighed at her wishful thinking, but knew there was no point, Della hated the thought of being with a man. She'd never told anybody, but as a 14 year old she'd suffered at the hands of one and it had put her off for life. Let them all think she was weird, she didn't care, though she had to admit, Patrick was different.

'Who are you gawping at, Miss Nosey Knickers?'
Her mammy asked as she joined her on the steps.

Daisy giggled, 'your man, Patrick King over there.
Honestly, mammy, he has a terrible tongue. He
knows all the best swear words when he hurts
himself, and I don't think he's ever sited a trailer
before in his life!'

Della laughed then, 'excuse me, madam, but a
young woman like yourself shouldn't know *any* of
the best swear words at all, young lady, but you're
right, I doubt Patrick has done this before, but he
has to start somewhere I guess. Hey, Daisy, what
about that trailer though? It must have cost him an
absolute fortune! I had a peep through the
windows earlier and all the furniture inside is still
covered in plastic, it's gorgeous, all cream leather
and white. Wouldn't last two minutes with my
brood though, can you imagine?'

Daisy nodded. 'I gave him cousin Aiden's number,
remember, so he's actually got me to thank for all
his fancy interior. I never found out what it cost
him, but knowing our Aiden, it wouldn't have
been a bargain.'

She didn't feel envious, never had in her life. Hers
had been a happy childhood in the main, despite
the lack of money or space. She simply liked to see
the finer things and vowed that some day, she too
would have a beautiful trailer like the one going in
opposite them.

She'd seen Patrick around quite a lot lately and
knew that her mammy and aunty Violet were
friends with him, but there was something about
him that intrigued her. He had this soft way about
him, and he always treated her with respect
whenever they'd spoken to each other, not like any
of the other men she knew on the site, and he
showed an interest in the women and children. Not
in a creepy way like some of them, but always had
a smile and time for a kickabout with the little lads,
and was always very respectful to her mammy.

'He's a nice man, isn't he, mammy?' Daisy asked,
'does this mean Patrick will be living up here from
now on?'

'He sure will,' her mammy answered as she
stroked her hair, 'and yes, my chickadee, he's a
lovely man. He'll make someone a lovely husband
one day.'

Daisy sighed and suddenly felt sad as she thought about Mirela. She'd adored the girl and thought of her as a little sister - even though there'd barely been an age difference, but now she was gone, never to come back. Daisy understood about death, she knew it was final, and although her parents had tried to hide most of the horrible circumstances from her, she'd found out about it. Daisy knew a lot of things her parents assumed she didn't. From being a small child she'd learned the art of becoming almost invisible.

It worked in her favour to keep quiet and not cause any trouble because it meant that people rarely took any notice of her, and this meant she saw and heard a lot of things. Things that she kept to herself and never told a living soul, but it meant she learned a lot about people. Over the years she perfected her skill and soon she was adept at reading others simply by watching them. She knew who was mean, she knew who the sneaky, sly ones were, and she knew a good soul when she met one. That's what Patrick was, she decided. Good to look at too, she acknowledged as she blushed and turned away.

Daisy stood up from the steps and hugged Della, 'I like him too, mammy. He hurts inside but he still has time for everybody. I think he and I will get on like a house on fire. Can I have some of your soup now?'

She didn't notice the strange look her mammy gave her as she stepped inside to the chaos of their own little van, and as she sat at the table, waiting for her lunch, she smiled to herself as a plan started to formulate. She knew beyond a doubt that Patrick King was going to change things, she just didn't know how yet. Her mammy used to say that fate wasn't always set in stone and often needed a kick up the arse, well that's what Daisy intended to do. She would make herself indispensable to Patrick, before anyone else did.

At her age it was expected that she would be an excellent cook and cleaner, so she would go over there as soon as she'd finished her soup, and be the first to offer her services. It was high time she put the past behind her, forgot about the horrible men, and concentrated on getting to know one whom she knew was kind. He had to be special for her dear friend, Mirela to have fallen so hard for him.

Chapter 33

1992

Patrick grinned as Violet straightened his tie. She kissed his cheek and stepped back to admire the man who was about to marry her best friend's daughter. Their courtship had been as passionate as it had been unexpected, slow burning at first, but Violet had always told him that she had seen it coming a mile off. She'd said she saw the same look in Della's eyes as she had seen in her daughters on that horrible day when she had declared her love. In fact both Violet and Della knew that fate had brought the two of them together to end the misery both women had felt for years after losing Mirela.

"Oh, Patrick, you look so handsome,' the woman said, a tear running down her cheek, 'my Mirela will be smiling down on you both today for sure.' She quickly made a sign of the cross as she looked heavenwards, 'doesn't he look gorgeous, my daughter?'

Smiling, Patrick put his huge arms around Violet – the woman who had been more of a mother to him these last few years than his own ever had, and he hugged her tightly. 'I know she'd approve, Violet, she loved Daisy, didn't she? Are you absolutely sure you are on board with this and that you will be alright today?'

'Behave yourself!' Violet said, mock scolding her favourite boy, 'I couldn't be happier, and that's all I want for you. Both Della and me are thrilled for both of you, now go on, get out of here while I get my fancy clobber on. Go on out there with the men and have a drink to settle those nerves.'

'If you don't mind, Violet, would it be alright if I sit in here for ten minutes? You can go start getting ready, but I just want a few minutes to myself before I go out to the lads. You know what they're all like when it's a celebration, I won't have the chance to compose myself once I go out there.'

Violet laughed, 'compose yourself indeed! My boy, you take as long as you need, but today, like you said, is a celebration, so no maudlin, you hear me?'

He smiled while Violet trotted off to her bedroom but as soon as she was out of sight he reached into his overnight bag and grabbed the bottle of malt Whisky he had there. Taking a long swig, his thoughts turned to the events that had brought him to this day. Daisy Wright had been eighteen when he first moved onto the site She'd been allowed to go to school until she was 15, unlike most of the other girls, and was fast learning the way of the women.

How to cook for a whole family, how to clean for hours on end to keep a trailer spic and span, and ideally how to be submissive with the men to prepare her for the later life she'd been born into. But, just like his Mirela, Daisy would have none of that. Gob on legs, her mother, Della, always called her, and she wasn't wrong. By the time he'd got to know her, she reminded Patrick so much of Mirela that he couldn't help but be drawn to her. Daisy looked nothing like his first love, with her long, blonde hair and blue eyes, but her attitude towards the old customs was very similar.

He had wondered, like most who lived on the site had, why, at her age she had not yet settled down with a man, but after they had spent time together, and she had opened up to him about what had happened to her as a young girl, he could completely understand, and he had vowed to never let come to any harm again.

What she had told him, although it had angered him, had actually made their bond stronger. He had agreed to keep her secret and in turn, Daisy had agreed to move heaven and earth to please her man.

'Don't you dare be looking me up and down, Patrick King! I'm not a piece of fecking meat!' were the first words Daisy had really spoken to him, and it was those words that had him attracted to her. He'd come home unexpectedly early that day and was surprised to see her lounging on his sofa with a glass of water. Before that exchange he hadn't even thought about fancying her, to him, she was just Della's daughter.

An Irish traveler who had cheekily told him that he'd be sorry if he didn't employ her as his cleaner and who'd then worked for him every day since. She was brilliant too, always kept out of his way, never interfered and he always came home to a sparkling trailer and a meal prepared for him. For four years she'd gone practically unnoticed. By the time she was 23 however, and Patrick 22, they were a couple.

They tried to keep it quiet at first because Patrick knew that although he'd lived on site for a few years now, and was generally accepted as one of their own, he was still technically a gorger, and the same rules applied to Daisy as they had to Mirela – they were expected to marry travelers.

Della's daughter however, had other ideas, and she wasn't afraid to voice them. No one was going to tell her who she could and couldn't be with, and to hell with the consequences. For years, Daisy had been teased about becoming an old maid, but still she hadn't bowed down and found a mate. She would be ready when she was good and ready and not a minute before. It was a good job her mother was of the same mind, and not afraid to stand up to her own husband, or things might have turned out differently.

Patrick couldn't put it off any longer. He was marrying Daisy Wright in just over an hour and outside, waiting for him, were a group of friends and a few bottles of Scotch. It was time to put melancholy thoughts behind him, the past was the past now, and he was truly thankful for the things Daisy had done to help him get over his grief. It was now time to repay her and give her the kind of marriage she had always dreamed of, and time to join his friends to toast their upcoming wedding. This would never be the kind of true love he'd felt for Mirela, but he had strong, protective feelings for her, and he knew they would be a good team for life, and that was enough. She was good in the sack too, he admitted to himself, none of that no sex before marriage shite from his Daisy.

'Time to fucking partayyyy!' He yelled, as he stepped out of Violet's trailer, swinging his bottle of best Whisky above his head to the sounds of cheers and clapping, 'my last hour of freedom, boys, let's get slaughtered.'

His best friend, and soon to be best man, Brendan Boyd, slapped him on the back, laughing as he yelled, 'we can get slaughtered, lads, but big lad here can only have a couple otherwise young Daisy Wright-Hook will put him to the floor the minute she has that ring on her finger.'

Everybody laughed and the drink flowed for half an hour before the men, seeing wives and girlfriends beckoning from various trailer doors, had to go put the finishing touches to their suits and boots and then make their way down to St Joseph's church. Patrick glanced over at Della's trailer but knew he wouldn't catch a glimpse of Daisy.

She'd be there now, sitting nervously in her dress, waiting for all the men to leave in their cars, before she'd step out herself to get into the trimmed up Rolls Royce that her dad and uncle had arranged for her. Apparently, it was serious bad luck to see his bride before she joined him at the alter, and Patrick had had enough of that to last a lifetime he decided as he ran to catch his best man up.

'It's fucking freezing out there! You're so lucky, lad,' Brendan said as they entered Patrick's spacious, modern trailer, rubbing his shirt sleeved arms briskly with his hands, 'I still can't get over the fact that you actually own this, and now to be getting married as well, a Christmas wedding no less, you've got it all, mush.'

Patrick laughed, 'and I see you're picking up the gypsy twang, boy, you'll soon be wanting a van of your own up here. Best be quick, lad, it's your job to get me to the church on time, as the old song goes.'

He left his friend to put on his jacket and style his hair as he went to the bathroom to do the same. Brendan Boyd had lived on Canterbury estate all his life, the same as Patrick, but they'd never moved in the same circles until Patrick had taken on the scrapyard. They'd become best mates over the last few years when Patrick had realized what an asset Brendan was, with his quick mind and his even faster fists. Coming from a large family and abject poverty as his dad was a prolific gambler, Brendan had jumped at the chance to be Patrick's right hand man. There wasn't a drug dealer left in Bradford who would dare to rip the pair off these days, and to Patrick, that meant something. One day he would set him up in his own trailer, he'd help his mate like Mick Keenan had helped him years ago, but it would be at the scrapyard, not on the site. One gorger was one too many in some people's opinion.

As he shook hands with as many guests as he could, Patrick saw his mother, waving frantically to get his attention. She was sitting on the front pew, alongside his father, and when he finally got to them, both stood to hug him. Things had been strained over the last year, especially with his dad, but it meant a lot to him that they were both here. Wild horses couldn't have kept his mam away, but he hadn't been certain his old man would turn up.

'Thanks for coming, dad,' he said, smiling, 'it means a lot. We'll have a good catch up afterwards down at the Vic, alright?'

His dad nodded and turned away, leaving Patrick free to gush generously about his mam's choice of outfit. A bright yellow fitted dress, with matching kitten heeled sandals. The middle of December too, but she'd still took off her black fur coat so that everybody could delight in her attire. Maureen always stood out like a sore thumb, but revelled in the recognition.

'Thanks, son,' she said, 'I look a damn sight better than some of them gypsy women, don't I?'

Patrick glanced around, embarrassed, 'give it a rest, mam, for a day, will you.' He hissed, 'we're in a church for fuck's sake!'

Before she could say anything else to show him up, he walked to join his best man, waiting for him at the alter.

'Isn't she fucking gorgeous?' Patrick whispered to Brendan as the music started and they turned to watch Daisy walking down the aisle, her father on one arm and her younger brother, Del, on the other. She smiled, shyly, as she noticed her groom staring, causing Patrick to feel butterflies in his stomach. She really was stunning at any time, but today, in her satin and lace, white gown and veil, with her blonde hair curled and piled high on her head, she almost took his breath away. Even so, he cast his eyes upwards as he turned back to the alter, and mentally prayed that Mirela was definitely okay with this. He knew she would be, of course, she still guided his every move.

Chapter 34

1995

Patrick emerged from his trailer into the hot August sunshine and smiled at the sight of his wife playing chase with their son. Little Daniel was almost three now, and had more energy than anyone Patrick knew. He was non stop from the moment he opened his eyes till he finally fell to sleep at around 8.00pm. If he was being honest, Patrick loved it when he had long days at work. He didn't know how Daisy coped with him all the time.

'Where's my boy?' Patrick yelled, his arms open wide to catch his boy as he ran and jumped at him.

'Here I am, daddy!' He yelled, 'I'm your boy!'

'Well, I think you just might be,' Patrick teased, 'let me have a good look at you, what's your name?'

'Little Danny King, daddy, I'm your boy, I am.'

'And if you're my boy, and I'm your daddy, what's my name then?'

Daniel raised his fists into the air and yelled, 'you're Patrick Lee King, the gypsy king!'

Patrick had added the name Lee to his in honour of Mirela and Violet, not long after the wedding, and Daisy had always been happy about it. After all, she'd loved Mirela too and had known her all her life. Violet hadn't been too sure about it at first, fearing it would remind people of Bo Lee, a name she had put firmly in the past, but she understood why it was important to Patrick. Daisy smiled and put her arms out to the little boy.

'You're such a clever wee boy,' she said, leaning in to kiss Patrick as she retrieved Daniel from him, 'and now that daddy's up and ready, we can go inside and cook some breakfast. Extra sausage for our little sausage, okay?'

'None for me, babes,' Patrick said, 'I'm going to grab something from the Tuck Inn, I promised Mick Keenan I'd call in on him this morning, he wants me to have the codes for the safes.'

Daisy smiled, 'you're a good friend to that fella, Patrick, I hope he realizes that. How is he doing?'

Mick had recently had another stroke and was now bed ridden. He could barely speak coherently, and according to his daily nurse, he was now pissing and shitting himself. For all the so called friends Mick had accumulated throughout the years, all the people he had helped out financially and otherwise, it sickened Patrick that none of them went to see him anymore.

They did in the beginning, most no doubt wondering what was happening with all of his money, but they soon fizzled out when they learned that only Patrick was trusted to take care of his affairs.

Patrick shook his head sadly, 'not good, babes. I don't think he'll be around for much longer to be honest, and I think he'll welcome the end. It must be fucking awful for him to be in that state. That scrap yard was his life, and it kills him to be trapped in his house like a fucking cabbage.'

'God bless him,' Daisy said as she made the sign of the cross, 'well, if he needs me to do any bits for him, shopping or cleaning or something, tell him he only has to say the word and I'll be there. Honestly, Patrick, I mean it, darling, just tell him that.'

Patrick kissed her and then his son, 'I will, mate,' he said, 'and I'll see the both of you later on. I'll be home for tea time. See you later, babes.'

He then checked his watch and jumped into his Landrover. His Daisy could cook a mean roast dinner but she was shit at a greasy breakfast, he'd call at the café before going to Mick's house, he had plenty of time, and the little bird behind the counter at the Tuck Inn always threw some extra toast and mushrooms on his plate.

He'd maybe repay the favour to her someday as she clearly fancied the pants off him. Daisy was his wife, and he loved her absolutely, but, he was only a man after all, and he faced temptation on a daily basis. He knew it was only a matter of time before he broke his vows, but it wouldn't mean anything, he also knew that.

He winced at the smell when he let himself into Mick's bedroom. The poor fucker must have shit himself again. Well as much as he loved him, there was no way he was offering to change his bastard nappy. He'd just have to pretend he couldn't smell it and hope that the nurse turned up soon.

'Morning, Mick!' He said as he sat down on the armchair beside the bed, 'how you doing, mate? Can I get you anything, a cup of tea?'

'A Whisky, pal,' Mick slurred, 'before that fucking nurse gets here.'

Patrick laughed and went into the kitchen, coming back with two large Whisky's, 'here you go, mate,' he said, putting a glass to his friend's lips, 'don't be fucking choking on it though, they'll have me done for murder, steady on.'

Mick slurped the whole measure and then tried to shuffle up the bed to a seated position but his arm let him down.

'Hang on, mate,' Patrick said, standing to hook his arms under Mick's, 'let me help you up.' He managed to lift him easily, his friend only weighing around 9 stone these days, and plumped up two pillows behind his back. 'That alright?'

Mick nodded and then reached out to grasp Patrick's hand. 'You know he's coming home, don't you?' He rasped, 'you gonna be alright, lad?'

Patrick hung his head for a moment. Bo lee had done almost two thirds of his fifteen years and reliable information had told him that his release was imminent. He nodded slowly and raised his head, 'you know I'll be alright, Mick, we've always talked about it, I'll be fine. Everything will be fine.'

He wondered how Mick knew about the release date. It didn't take a genius to work out mind, it was standard practice to be let out at this stage of a sentence if you'd kept your head down and not fucked up, but Mick seemed to know for sure.

'Who told you?' He asked, 'and do you know exactly when?'

Mick shook his head, 'don't know the date, but it's soon,' he said, obviously struggling to talk and keep breathing, 'Titch Williams sent me a card. He wrote it in that. Cunt! Must have kept in touch with him.'

'Well, fuck him,' Patrick said, 'and the rats that have been writing to him. Mind you, it's because they have that we've been able to keep tabs, so, every cloud, as they say.'

Mick looked hard at Patrick as though searching for something deeper from him before speaking again. 'I'll shut my trap about it now, lad,' he finally said, 'because we've got business to sort out, but you do realise how much your little Danny looks just like the cunt, don't you? Let's hope that none of them have told him that much.'

Patrick said nothing. His son was his whole life, and if he was honest, the fact that he shared Bo Lee's black wavy hair and deep, dark eyes, gave him some satisfaction. Fate had obviously shuffled up the gene pool to ensure that the past would never be forgotten, and he didn't want to forget it, not yet. Nobody had ever passed comment about Danny's looks before, not even Daisy or Violet, they wouldn't dare, but Mick got a pass due to how close they were and because of his ailing health.

He spent the next hour patiently listening to Mick as he told him the combination codes to his four safes. None of it could be written down, he had to store it all in his head, the codes, the names and addresses, the amounts folk owed, the ones to watch out for and the ones who could be trusted. All vital information for a business such as theirs. The man wanted to ensure that Patrick knew it all, inside and out.

'I don't have long left, kid,' Mick gasped, 'but you get everything, and I mean that. I've got no one else, so no one's going without, don't you worry. You carry on doing what you're doing, and nobody can touch you. It's all yours, Patti.'

Patrick couldn't help himself, he gave a huge gulp as the tears started. No one, other than his mother, had called him Patti for years, and no one had looked after him like this man had. It didn't seem fair that he didn't have long for this life and it must be shit for him not to have any family to be with him as he neared the end. The rest of his mates had all fucked off weeks ago too, when it became apparent that there was nothing in it for them. This was all just too much to take.

'Stop that, soft lad,' Mick said, patting Patrick's hand, 'or I'll change my mind and leave it all to the fucking cat's home. You've earned it, lad, and that young 'un of yours will inherit it from you no doubt, get him started in the game as soon as he's fit for it, Patti, like you did. I imagine there's nothing better than a father teaching his son the tricks of the trade.'

'Thanks, Mick, and don't worry, my lad will be there alongside me every step of the way.' Patrick said, scrubbing at his face, 'you've been like a dad to me, you know that, and I swear to you, I won't let you down. I'll make sure you live on in everything I do.'

Patrick meant every word of his promise. Over the last few years, he and Mick had spent hours making plans for the future, and he intended to honour Mick by carrying out every last one of his wishes. As he drove up to the scrap yard, he smiled at the bright future he had ahead. Thanks to Violet, he was recognized now as a Gypsy King, fuck, even his name should have been a clue to the title he'd one day hold. But this King hadn't even started his rise to the top yet and the other one had already hit the bottom. The king is dead, long live the king! Patrick grinned at his own analogy.

Chapter 35

Maureen King carried a tray of drinks in from the kitchen, little Daniel pushing her from behind, giggling.

'You got a squishy bum bum, nanny,' he yelled gleefully, 'it feel like my play doughs!'

'Cheeky little sod!' Maureen chastised as she set the tray down and passed Daisy a mug of coffee. 'It's not the cheap stuff,' she said as she noticed Daisy wrinkle her nose, 'It's that new one off the adverts, really nice.' She took the blue, plastic sippy cup and handed it to her grandson, 'and this one's for you, cheeky monkey, and it's blackcurrant, so careful not to spill it on nanny's carpet.'

'Thank you, fatty bum bum,' Daniel said as he took the cup and promptly shook it, spilling juice all over the coffee table.

'Stop being cheeky,' Daisy scolded, 'or mammy will smack your hand, naughty boy, and careful with that bloody cup.'

'Oh, he's alright,' Maureen said, generously. This kid could do anything as far as she was concerned, he was her second shot at life and she loved him with a passion she'd never felt for her own two. Even though her Patti barely brought him round, she was so grateful that his wife did.

The only fly in the ointment was that Big Pat didn't share her enthusiasm. He was never mean to the boy or anything, but he simply didn't love him like she did. Patti was one thing, he loved him for sure, but this beautiful child looked too much like the man he hated and there was nothing she could do about that.

'What's troubling you, Daisy?' She said, 'because you look like you've got ants in your pants.'

Daniel was now absorbed in playing with an assortment of construction vehicles from his toy box, leaving the women to chat for ten minutes, and although Violet would have much preferred to engage with the boy, she knew she'd have to listen to his mother moan about this, that and the other first. 'Come on,' she said, 'spit it out. Has my boy been giving you grief or something, because I'll have a word if he has. It's all frigging work with that kid, no time for anything else. He'll end up like bleeding Mick Keenan if he isn't careful.'

'Oh, Maureen, don't say that,' Daisy said, 'I don't mind all that, I love that he's a hard worker. No, it's just, I don't know, but lately it's like he's got something on his mind that he isn't sharing with me, and that's not like him. He's distant, somehow.' She sighed and took a drink of her coffee, 'I don't know, Mo, maybe it's just me, overthinking as usual.'

Maureen laughed, 'honestly, you young girls. Our bloody Danni is just the same. Thinks her bloke should tell her everything.' She leaned towards Daisy, 'listen, love, in all the years I've been married to Pat, I've never once asked him about his business. It's not our concern, love, trust me. So long as they are good providers – and I know my boy is, then you shouldn't question it. Look, Daisy, I've known men leave their women when they become too pushy. Our job is to look pretty, bring up the kids and that's that. Everything else, especially work, is to be left alone. Our Patti is old school, just like his dad, that's all it is, love.'

Daisy took a sip of her coffee and set it straight back down, 'I'm sorry, Mo, I can't drink that,' she said, 'I know it's the good stuff, but I can only drink tea since Daniel was born.'

Maureen's face lit up, 'you pregnant again, girl? Only I know what you gypsies are like for having babies, like bleeding rabbits you are! I went right off my coffee when I was up the duff.'

'No, I'm not,' Daisy said, 'I'd have one every bloody year if my mother had her way, but it's because of her that I intend to keep a small family. Maybe one more in a year or so and that's it, it won't be like mammy's trailer, everyone always fighting for a bit of space.'

Disappointed, Maureen snatched away the offending coffee cup and marched back to the kitchen to make tea. Trust her lad to marry a gypsy who *didn't* want a tribe of kids. Well, she intended on having a word with Patti all the same. It would be his decision on how many babies to have, not Daisy's. She'd never felt such love before, and little Danny had been a gift, a new lease of life, and she wanted more.

'Did you know Bo Lee was coming out?' Daisy asked as she accepted her fresh cup, 'I'm wondering if that's what causing Patrick to be a bit different. Has he said anything to you?'

Maureen pursed her lips and folded her arms, her son had said plenty to her about that twat over the years, none of which she would discuss with this girl. 'Nope, not a peep,' she lied, scooping little Daniel up into her arms, 'come on, baby, let's go look in nanny's fridge, see if we can find some goodies for you.'

Daniel squealed happily and kissed Maureen sloppily on the lips, 'I love you, nanny,' he said, 'you my best mate.'

* * *

Bo Lee reached beneath his mattress and pulled out the letter for what must have been the 20th time. His cell mate, Skunky Sam, was somewhere on the wing getting stoned, so it gave Bo the chance to really try to study the words. Before prison, he'd never been able to read or write, but thanks to an insistent education officer, he was now quite proficient. Unlike the sender of the letter – Chrissy Lee, whose spelling was that bad, it took Bo at least three reads to decipher it.

Hope this letter finds you well, Bo, and that you're looking forward to getting out. I'm gut sorry I've not kept in touch, but I have a new life now, down in Peterborough, with a wife and 3 chavvies. My eldest, John Boy Lee has writ this letter for me so forgive the scrawl. I just want to let the past lie, Bo, and us all to move on. Me and James Michael have a guttering business, he's moved down with us all, and we want you to join us. You'll never guess what, James Michael's sister married that fucking girlie boy, that Jimmy Jackson! Anyway, we don't see anything of them anymore and that suits me fine. It's us that are family Bo, and that comes first, not what's happened before. I know you won't go back to Bradford and I don't blame you. We don't ever have to go back there again. I will find out your release date, Bo, and I'll be there on that morning to pick you up and take you home and I hope you'll come. See you soon, Bo, your nephew, Chrissy Lee.

For the first five years inside, Bo Lee had been a broken man. Traumatised by the fact he had killed his own daughter, and simply unable to face the terrible truth that for 16 years he'd had a son that he never knew existed. The prison doctor had insisted that Bo be transferred straight to the psychiatric unit – known as the 'Ding Wing', during his first week, and he ended up spending two years on there, enjoying the oblivion that the powerful drugs he was given afforded him.

When he was finally able to allow himself to speak to the doctors, it had been a very long, very tough journey before he was ready to join the land of the living, back in general population, and even then he wasn't right. He knew he'd never be the man he once was, and like the coiled spring he was, it only took a wrong look or a wrong word from a fellow inmate, before he either broke down and shut down, or lashed out violently and would end up on a week's bang up – locked away, like an animal in isolation with only one hour a day of solitary exercise.

Now, almost ten years in, Bo Lee was a different kind of animal. A gentle giant, the more sensible inmates would say, whilst others who weren't quite brave enough, would say he was a pussy cat, behind his back. Skunky Sam, his pad mate of 18 months knew that Bo had mellowed over his time, but he also knew about the nightmares that kept the man awake at night, the screams of terror when he couldn't wake himself up, and he knew that deep down, Bo Lee was no pussy cat, he had a beast inside of him just waiting for the right stick to poke it awake. He walked back into the cell just as Bo was putting his letter back in place.

'You'll wear the ink off that fucking thing,' he said, grinning as he leapt onto his bunk, 'the words won't change you know, pal, the more you fucking read it. The boy is coming to collect you, Bo, you go with him if you want, you don't if you have other plans, it's that simple.'

Bo Lee nodded thoughtfully, 'I know, Skunky, and it's good of him, it's just something I never expected, you know, after everything. He had just as much reason to blame me for it all as everyone else did.'

'Look, Bo, from what you've told me, that lad never had anything to do with those you lived with. He's your brother's lad, and like they say, blood's thicker than water, mate, he's your family. You need a fresh start and he's there offering you one, bite his fucking hand off, mate, a new home, new job, family around you, what's to question?'

Bo shook his head and stood up, sighing, 'I dunno, mush. It's been a long time, is all, and whilst I've been stuck in here, everyone else has moved on. The lad was a conniving little fucker when I last saw him, and now he's a family man with three chavvies and his own business. I suppose it's the same for everyone who's done a big chunk, I'm just overthinking everything.' He sighed before making his mind up, 'fancy an hour in the gym, Skunk? Gotta get rid of some of this fucking flab if I'm to be working on the gutters in less than a week, eh?'

Skunky laughed, 'you're joking aren't you? I'm off me fucking bonce, mate! You go, I'll get an hour's kip before tea. If you hurry up, you'll just catch the nonces coming out. Be able to give 'em a bit of shit, that'll sort your head out.'

'Can't afford to get myself into any shit now, Skunky boy,' Bo said, 'need to be a proper saint if I don't want any more time, don't I?'

Peterborough, Bo mused as he pushed the 150 pound bars. He'd been there before, years ago to buy a truck from a traveler his brother had put him on to, and it was far enough away from Bradford so that the past wouldn't keep hitting him in the face. Right then, Bo decided, that's where he'd go. The probation service wanted him to carry on seeing some kind of shrink once he was on the out, but fuck that, they'd have to find him first. He made his way down to the gymnasium, careful to avoid eye contact with the nonces – who were, as Skunky had said, just leaving. It wouldn't do to batter someone's head in this close to his release date no matter how much he detested them.

Chapter 36

Patrick reluctantly came out of the bathroom, hoping his wife had calmed down a bit. He'd pissed her off this morning and hiding out in the bog for a bit was the only escape when Daisy King was sulking. The council had recently been on the site building some new facilities for the community. A large kitchen that anyone could use, a new shower block and a large double sized shed that was meant to be used as an education block. Twice weekly, a teacher from the local school came up, and any children that wanted to, could go and do some lessons with them.

Parents were meant to encourage it, but travelers, being as they were had actively gone against it. Within a fortnight, the teacher had stopped trying. The new building was great, but they were having no nosey teachers up there, not a chance, and the women had other plans for that building, one of which was why Daisy was now having an argument with her husband.

'You knew it was today, Patrick,' she shouted, 'I must have told you a million times that the playgroup is every Friday morning, and today's the first one. Why the hell would you want to take Daniel with you today of all days?'

'So what!' Patrick yelled back, 'what the fuck does it matter if he misses the first one, it's not like it'll be any different to any other day. He'll still be playing with the same little scratters he's always playing with, I don't see what the problem is.'

'The problem, Patrick,' Daisy said, clearly trying to keep calm, 'is that we all spent a long time preparing that place, we organized a rota, me and the other women, for when we'd supervise and what not. Today is my shift, and Daniel was looking forward to it. And besides, you're always working, you never spend time with him on Fridays, why does it have to be today you go to your mam's with him?'

Patrick couldn't be arsed explaining himself any further. He picked Daniel up from the sofa and set him down on the floor.

'Go on, mate,' he said, 'go get your coat. Nanny Maureen is making us bacon and eggs and we don't want to be late.'

While Daniel trotted off to his bedroom, Patrick tried to soothe things over with his wife, 'come on, babe, stop being mad with me,' he said as he stroked Daisy's hair, 'he only gets to see my mam once a week, and she really dotes on him, you know that. You can still go do your teacher bit down at the sheds, just let me have some time with our boy, I never get to do this, and I promised my mam so she'll have made plans and stuff.'

He smiled when Daisy laughed. Her quick temper dissipating as usual when he soft soaped her.

'Teacher bit!' She said, 'I'll be more like a fecking zoo keeper and you know it.' She sighed, 'alright then, take him to your mam's and let him have some fun I suppose, I'll just tell the women he'll start our nursery next week. I was just so excited for him that's all, honestly Patrick we've got all sorts down there. Sand, water play, colouring and painting stuff, play dough and loads of toys, he'd love it.'

'I know, babes,' Patrick laughed, 'I paid for it all! But listen, he won't miss out, I promise you. I'll make sure he has a great day with me and my mam, we might take him into town or something as well, and all that stuff, down at the *nursery* will still be there next week.'

'I suppose so,' Daisy said, hugging him, 'it's a good job I love you, Patrick Lee King, because no other man on this earth would tell me what to do. Now go on, piss off the pair of you, before I change my mind.'

As Patrick, with Daniel safely strapped into the Landrover, made the short journey down to his mam's, he thought about what Daisy had said. The truth was that she had always done what he'd wanted, no arguments, no questions asked. Daisy had played a huge part in Patrick being accepted into the community, and had helped build him into the man he now was.

It was the main reason he had married her, and Daisy knew this. She loved him unconditionally and had no expectations other than for him to be a good dad to their son, and to provide her with another child when she was ready. Patrick had always been happy with the arrangement and he knew that his Mirela would give her blessing, especially given how much the girl had done for him over the years.

Ten minutes later they were enjoying a fry up at his mam's and Maureen was in her element to have them both there, all to herself.

'You want a couple more sausages, son?' She asked as she dropped a third one onto little Daniel's plate, 'they're not the cheap supermarket crap, I got these from the butcher, he makes 'em special for me.'

'I'm fine, mam, I think frigging five sausages is enough for anyone, and please don't give the little fella any more, he'll eat till you stop feeding him that one.'

'Nothing wrong with a good appetite,' she said, 'he's a growing lad, aren't you, little man? You're going to be big and strong just like your daddy!'

'I am, nanny,' Daniel replied, his mouth stuffed full, 'I be big, like daddy, mammy said I not gonna be mouthy like nanny.'

Patrick grinned, sheepishly, as his mother began to scowl, 'she never said it like that, mam, it was just when he was swearing, she said it as a joke, to me, not him.'

He left Maureen to fuss and chat to Daniel as he finished his breakfast whilst he thought about his plans for the day ahead. His mother wouldn't care a jot that he intended on leaving the boy with her while he went about his business, in fact she'd prefer it, he knew that, and he had a busy schedule in front of him today, one which he couldn't deviate from. Today's job would ensure that he and his little family wouldn't ever have to worry about anything.

Obviously, he had kept his plans from Daisy, that girl stressed out far too much about anything illegal these days. He knew of course that it was since they'd had little Danny, that had changed everything for her. From that day to this she had insisted that all his dealings be on the straight and narrow, she daren't risk Patrick going to jail, leaving her boy without a daddy.

'Is everything still where it was in my old room?' he asked, 'I just need to get something from my box. You're alright minding our Daniel aren't you while I go get some work done?'

'Course I'm alright,' Maureen said, her face softening, 'I'll take him to the park for a bit, and yes, love, your stuff is all where you left it. I've told you before, no one will go in that room until madam allows my grandson to sleep over, and then it'll be his. I don't know why you can't have a word and sort it out. It's not fair on the boy.'

'And I've told you, mam, it's for no other reason than the way my dad is. Till he can prove he bears no grudges, we're not leaving him here. And it's not Daisy's decision, so don't go blaming her, I'll be the one who decides when and where the boy sleeps out.'

Patrick left his mam grumbling as he went up to retrieve the photo he wanted from the box beneath his old bed. It was the only photograph he had of Mirela and it had been playing on his mind recently that it was becoming harder to picture her as time went by, and he needed to remember.
 For six months he had shut down and couldn't bear to replay the events of that day in his mind, but slowly he had taught himself to allow fragments of memory to permeate his thoughts, and gradually it got easier. Now, it was like an old movie he had watched, and in his head he could watch it from start to horrible end without getting upset. The overriding emotion was anger, but no longer uncontrollable, it was now strangely comforting, and as much a part of every day as his evening meal.

He sat on the edge of the bed as he gazed lovingly at the photograph. Mirela's eyes seemed to be staring right at him, her long, black curls framing her lovely face, and she was laughing. A close up snap of her, that Della had taken years earlier, she was standing beneath a tree and looked like she didn't have a care in the world. Patrick carefully placed the photograph inside his wallet and smiled. Now he had both loves of his life, side by side in the little plastic slots. Mirela and his Daniel.

'Nanny said fuckin' 'ell,' Daniel yelled, the minute Patrick walked back into the room, 'smack her bum, daddy, she naughty!'

'Well, he threw his bleeding tractor at my head,' Maureen shouted, 'little sod! He'll be the one getting a cracked arse if he isn't careful.'

Patrick grinned, knowing full well that his mother would sooner eat shit than lay a hand on her little angel. 'Hey you, monkey!' He chastised his son, 'daddy has to go now, but you be a good boy for nanny, you hear, or she'll be smacking your bum and I mean it.'

Daniel leapt up at Patrick to kiss him goodbye, 'I be good, you got 'portant work, daddy?'

Patrick glanced at his mam and smiled, 'I have, kid, very important work, but I'll be back to pick you up later. Now be a really good boy and I might bring you a present back.'

Ten minutes later, Patrick was emerging onto the M62 to get to his meeting. Little did Daniel know, but this was to be the most important job of his life. Today would change everything and Patrick had never been more ready for it. He turned up the music to drown out his thoughts. All the thinking and planning had been done already and he didn't want any doubts creeping in. As much as he would enjoy what was to come this day, he wanted it to be over so that he could get back to his life without any worrying.

Chapter 37

Chrissy Lee stared at Michael James in disgust, 'can't you close your fucking mouth when you eat, mush? You're like a fucking animal!'

They were sitting in a transport café in Sheffield, just off the M1 motorway, eating burgers and chips, and Chrissy was beginning to feel paranoid. Driving to a prison, willingly, was an alien concept for starters, and that made him uneasy, and the contents of their van were questionable should they get a tug by the cops. All that and now his sackless mate was drawing unnecessary attention, slobbering like a dog with grease dripping down his unshaven chin.

'Everyone's staring at us for fuck's sake, you'd think you hadn't eaten for a week.'

'Oh, behave,' Michael James laughed, showing a mouthful of burger and ketchup, 'no one's staring at us, it's a fucking greasy spoon, not a posh restaurant, Chrissy, what's up with you, mate? Chill your fucking beans for god's sake and get that scran down your neck, you've hardly touched it.' Without looking up, he then wiped across his chin with the sleeve of his jacket, 'it's you that's having folk looking at us, you divvy.'

Chrissy scanned the café as he put down his fork. He'd lost his appetite and just wanted to get back on the road and get today over and done with. It had been many years since he'd seen his uncle and he was nervous at the thought of it. If he was being honest with himself, Bo Lee had actually done him a solid, shooting Mirela back then. It had solved all his problems as he'd never wanted to marry the bird from the off. It had been his dad and uncle who'd arranged it all, and to save aggro, he'd simply gone along with it.

It was expected that he take a wife and to him, this took all the effort out of searching for a suitable one. She'd been a pretty girl on the face of it, and he would have enjoyed bedding her now and again, but the fucking mouth on her! That and the fact that her dad was Bo Lee had made him have second thoughts. So, whilst everybody else had been grieving and calling it a tragedy, Chrissy had been secretly thanking his stars that he'd had a lucky escape.

'Nothing's up with me,' he told his friend, 'it's just the thought of seeing him after all this time. I wonder if he's still as scary as I remember him. He might not even be there, mush, might have had a better offer. On that letter I told him, no worries if he didn't want to show.'

'He'll be there, and he's probably a right fat bastard now,' Michael James said, 'either that or fit as fuck. They go one way or the other in the nick, don't they? Depends if he's been looking after himself.' He laughed then, spitting half a chip out, 'anyway, what's it fucking matter?'

Chrissy shrugged, 'I don't suppose it does. Aren't you nervous though? What if he fucking hates us? I mean, neither have us have paid him a visit in all these years, he might have someone else coming to pick him up.'

Thankfully, Michael James picked up a napkin this time and wiped across his mouth, letting out a huge burp before answering, 'who? Who but us would travel all this way to pick up that fucker? Everyone else hates his guts, mush, he'll be glad to see us, just you watch and see.'

Chrissy grabbed his coat from the back of his chair and stood up to leave, 'come on then, charver,' he said, 'let's get off, we've still about an hour's drive left before we get there, it's just outside York according to our John Boy.'

'Proper little navigator that kid of yours,' Michael James laughed as he followed towards the carpark, 'he must have your dad's brains, lad, 'cos he certainly don't get them from you.'

'My dad's been in Full Sutton nick,' Chrissy recalled as they walked back to the van, 'years ago like, when I was a chavvy, he did five years for his part in an armed robbery, that's why me ma left him. Soon as he got out, she was off. Trouble was, the bitch left us with him and he had to go cap in hand to his brother Bo Lee for hand outs for a while. It was shit, man, we never had fuck all back then.'

'Ha! I wonder if Bo Lee realises that,' Michael James laughed, 'imagine if in his cell, he saw his brother's name scrawled on the wall, that would be really funny!'

Chrissy rolled his eyes as he climbed into the driver seat. As usual, Michael was completely missing the point, 'funny as fuck, ya gloit, get in the fucking van.'

* * *

Bo Lee took one last look around his pad. Everything he owned, all the stuff he'd built up over the years, he was leaving for Skunky, so it didn't really look any different. His only possessions were the prison issue plastic bag, containing his toothbrush, a bible, a few T-shirts and his baccy tin. Bo hadn't smoked when he went inside but once he learned that tobacco was the main currency, he'd started dealing in it. This, in turn had led him to take up the habit himself.

'You said all your goodbyes then, mate?' Skunky asked as he transferred the biscuits and cakes that Bo had given him to his own locker, 'not that you'll miss any of us fuckers, eh? We'll all be long forgotten the minute you set foot through those gates.'

'Said all I had to say last night,' Bo answered, 'like you said, there wasn't many I needed to speak with.' He smiled at his friend, the truth was, Skunky was the only one worth saying goodbye to. If it hadn't been for him, Bo knew he probably wouldn't be leaving today at all, he'd have had no chance keeping it together these last couple of years without his calming influence. Still, the man was most likely right, after today Bo would spend no time wondering about the inmates he would be leaving behind. 'I wonder who your new cell mate is, did they say?'

'Nah!,' Skunky said, 'I'm hoping they keep my pad as a single for a bit, be nice not to be smelling another fella's farts all night for a change.'

Bo laughed and then noticed the guard on the corridor outside, he tuned back to Skunky, 'right then, lad, that's me off,' he said, holding his hand out to shake, 'and remember, keep your head down and your nose clean.'

'Told you before, mate, mine is the cleanest snout in here, all that white stuff keeps it all nice and sparkly.' He gripped Bo Lee's hand and shook it, 'seriously, mate, I hope it all goes well for you. I hope that nephew is out there waiting, and you get your fresh start. Listen, if you get bored, write me a letter sometime. Another two years for me, it'll be nice to hear from you. I'll even send you a Visiting Order if you like.'

Bo laughed, he knew that Skunky was joking about the V.O. There was no way he would step back inside this place once he'd left. He slapped his friend on the shoulders and then left with the screw, Mr Michaels, to make their way down to reception for discharge. It was still quite early so the wings were pretty quiet for a change. For the first time in a long time, Bo wondered what the weather was like outside. Not that he hadn't been out in the yard or anything, he did that every day, but had never bothered what it was like. Sun, rain, snow or hail, it was all the same to a prisoner, an hour outside was an hour outside no matter what it was like. It was April now though, so it should be mild at least. He decided to make conversation with the officer. Mr Michaels was one of the few decent ones after all.

'So, is the sun shining for me then?' He asked, 'only a judge once told me it would be a cold day in Hell when I came out.'

The screw laughed, 'it's actually nice and warm, Bo, you'll not be needing a coat anyway. You got someone coming to pick you up, lad, or is transport taking you to a hostel?'

For prisoners like Bo, who had done a big chunk of time, they were offered the opportunity to go to a hostel for up to three months, to get themselves sorted. Give them the chance to find work and somewhere more permanent to live if they had no one on the outside.

A lot of ex convicts had lost everyone and everything during their lock up, so this kind of arrangement was the only option for them. For a long time, Bo Lee had thought he might have no choices when release day came, but thankfully he'd got his Hail Mary in the unexpected shape of his nephew.

'I'm all sorted, Mr Michaels,' Bo said, 'if all goes to plan anyway. My brother's lad is meant to be waiting for me, and I've got a place. I'll be alright.'

The nerves started to kick in as he waited to be signed out. Another officer was reading him his license conditions and one checked off the belongings he'd had confiscated on the day he went in. He was glad it was Michaels who patted him down, but still, his guts were churning, and he didn't know why.

He'd waited over ten years for this day, so now, why was he bricking it? Bo put it down to the not knowing what was to come. On the out, he'd always been a planner, always knew what was coming from one day to the next. Even in prison the routine had kept him settled, all this was getting him rattled. Finally, he was escorted to the gates, and there at the top of the long drive was a white Transit van. That had to be him.

Bo Lee sighed as he saw Chrissy and the Callaghan twin jump out of the van and walk towards him, smiling and grinning. All was well.

'Fuck me!' Bo yelled, 'come here you lads, look at the size of you both, fucking men you are now boys, eh?'

Both lads slapped Bo on the back, shook hands, and laughed along with him. 'You haven't changed a bit, uncle,' Chrissy said, 'well apart from the greys in your hair, what's all that about?'

Bo felt at ease now. These boys were family and no matter what had happened in the past, family was all that mattered, even if he never really liked them in the first place, they were here now. Familiar faces, the twang of the gypsy accent and the sight of a Transit van all served to settle Bo and made him feel the first stirrings of happiness. A feeling he hadn't had for years.

'Cheeky fucker!' Bo laughed as he reached out to clip Chrissy round the head, 'you might be a grown man now, but you're still young enough to get a hiding from me, mush.'

'Come on, let's get the fuck away from here,' Michael James said, 'gives me the heebie jeebies standing outside this place.'

'So,' Bo said, leaning over to the driver seat, once he was settled in the back of the van, 'Peterborough you say. Is it the same site the Doyles' live at? I once bought a truck from them.'

Chrissy glanced at Michael James before answering, 'yeah, Jimmy and Myra are still on there, so is young Kevin, the other two lads moved away though.'

Bo settled back onto his makeshift seat propped against one of the wheel arches, 'be a long drive from here then, lads, I might try get a bit of shut eye.' He bashed the back of the driver's seat, 'unless of course you boys want to yap my head off the whole journey?'

'No, no, uncle,' Chrissy Lee said, 'I don't need a catch up on tales from the big house, thank you. I've heard enough of those from my dad over the years. You get some sleep.'

He didn't know how long he'd been sleeping when he was disturbed by the back door opening. Sunlight streamed into the van causing Bo to squint and shade his eyes with a hand. 'We here already?' He asked, pulling himself up so he could get out, 'fuck me I must have slept for hours!'

Bo was puzzled as he couldn't see which of the lads had opened the doors and no one was answering him, but as soon as he jumped down, he realized immediately why his guts had been warning him all day. His face contorted as he saw who was standing outside, waiting for him. That face had haunted him for years, the face of himself as a young boy at first, but now, now it was the face of a man.

'Hello *dad*,' Patrick said, a smirk on his face.

Chapter 38

Bo Lee couldn't help but stare at the man. He was searching the face for some clue as to what was happening here. Everything he saw, the dark, angry eyes, the unflinching, set smirk, told him he was in danger.

'In case you're not quite following,' Patrick explained, 'those two hate your fucking guts too. They brought you to me.'

Bo looked to where Patrick was pointing and his face paled as he saw that both lads were now holding weapons. Chrissy a shotgun and Michael a crowbar. The two of them looked a lot less scary than the obvious man in charge, in fact they looked terrified. Still, Bo mused, two scared men with weapons were still dangerous men.

'What is all this?' Bo Lee finally asked, moving back towards the van so he could lean on it. He had to think fast if he were to live through this. 'You prepared to do what I've just done, lad? Ten fucking years or more, and for what? Revenge? Don't you think I've suffered enough?'

'Don't you fucking dare!' Patrick spat, walking closer to the van, 'you piece of shit. Don't you fucking dare say you've suffered, you cunt! You killed your fucking daughter, blasted her head to bits in cold blood, and you think you've fucking suffered enough?'

Bo was wise enough to know his enemy, he could feel his legs beginning to buckle and he could see that this was not going to be a walk in the park. This man – his own flesh and fucking blood, wanted to kill him. He knew that, and he needed to do something about it. He moved away from the van, forcing his legs to remain steady, and he turned to the cowards at the side, hoping they still feared him as much as they once did.

'You set this up, you pair of cunts?' He asked, arms splayed out, 'my own fucking family and you'd do this.' He swung back and pointed at Patrick, 'you owe him fuck all! None of us do, just tell him to fuck off and let's get going. No grudges held.'

Patrick laughed manically as he watched Chrissy and Michael squirming, and Bo watched the whole exchange. Something was wrong about this scene, why wasn't his so called son holding a gun? He didn't appear to have a weapon so it would be easy for the other lads to turn their weapons onto Patti, so why weren't they?

'Look lad, Patti it is, isn't it?' he said, 'I don't know what you've got on these two idiots, but whatever it is, you don't have to do this. I've done my time, and I live every day with the horror of what I did. To you, and my Mirela, I …'

'Shut, the fuck, up!' Patrick screamed, lunging at Bo and grabbing him by the neck, 'don't ever say her name in my presence, you hear me? You hear me? And the name's Patrick!'

Bo was scared now. For the first time in his life, he was shit scared, and suddenly and inexplicably, he felt something else alongside the fear. Pride. He stared into this man's eyes and knew without a doubt he was his son. Not just the way he looked, but everything about him. This man was self made. He was confident, fearless and brutal, much like himself. To his shame, he started to cry.

'I never knew you existed, son, I swear I didn't. Not till that day.' He said, 'But I know now, and I promise you, I want to be there for you. I don't blame you for all of this, I don't, I'd do exactly the same, but please, Patti, Patrick I mean, just give me the chance your mother never gave me. Let me make up for all the years I never knew I was your dad. Your real dad.'

Patrick let go of Bo's shirt collar and stared at him, 'you actually fucking mean that, don't you, you cunt? You actually think I could ever look at you and not see my Mirela with half her face fucking hanging off?' He started to scream at Bo hysterically now, 'I've waited ten bastard years for this day.' He suddenly reached into his pocket and pulled out two photographs. 'Look, look at them, cunt!' He shoved them into Bo's face.

Bo was half blinded by the salty tears now, but he reached for the photos and stared at them. He gave a huge gulp and thought he might stop breathing as he looked at his beloved Mirela, and then he studied the other one. A little boy, around the age of three, with the same black hair, the same dark eyes as his own. Surely this couldn't be…that baby had died in the womb, he'd heard that in prison. He held the photo towards the man who wanted to take his life. 'I don't know who this is,' he said, quietly.

Patrick snorted, 'no, you don't. And you never will,' he said, 'that's my son, Daniel Lee King, your fucking grandson. The one that didn't die in his mother's womb.' He snatched both photos away from Bo Lee and put them back into his pocket. 'And just so you know, before you take your final fucking nap, I married the first gypsy girl I set eyes on, just to have this day. To have a Lee son, something you'd never have, and to take your title of gypsy king. All so I could meet you here today and show you what I've fucking taken from you.'

Bo was now resigned to the fact he was going to die. Everything the boy was saying made twisted sense somehow, and he knew his fate was sealed. What he still couldn't understand though was why his nephew, Chrissy, was holding the gun, why wasn't Patti going to murder him himself. There had to be more to this.

'You look confused,' Patrick said, summoning the two lads across with his hand, 'well let me explain. This cunt, here,' he pointed to Chrissy Lee, 'he terrorized my Mirela, tried to fucking rape her on her 15th birthday, while you and your fucking cronies were partying, he then followed her about like some kind of fucking spy.' He then pointed to Michael James, 'and this fucking divvy also made her life a misery. He knew about all of it, the nasty cunt, and failed to tell you or Violet. Both of them had it coming, I just had to find a way to make it worth my while.'

Bo looked at his nephew, 'what's he talking about?' he asked, 'is all this true that you hurt my daughter?'

Chrissy hung his head, but still kept a tight grip on the gun he was holding. 'I never meant to hurt Mirela, Bo, it was just grabbing and fucking about. We were betrothed. But that's not what he has on us. That's not why we have to do this.'

Bo might be about to die but he was still enraged by what he was hearing, 'well what then? He yelled, willing to risk a shot as he walked towards the pair of cowards, 'I can understand why *he* wants to do it, but why are you two involved? And why the fuck would either of you hurt my daughter? If I make it through this day, I'll kill the pair of you, I swear I will.'

'Let me clear it up for you,' Patrick said, walking towards them all, 'first of all, you definitely won't make it through this day, and secondly, see these two didn't just hurt my Mirela, did you lads?' He grinned as Chrissy and Michael James looked like they were about to throw up, 'no, it seems they have a thing for underage girls, and my Daisy…' he turned to Bo, 'you remember little Daisy, don't you? Della Wright's eldest lass. Anyway, oh, and Daisy is my wife by the way, in case you're interested, the mother of little Daniel Lee.'

Bo listened in shock as Patrick went on to tell the whole story.

'She was a broken woman when we met,' he said, 'hiding a secret since she was just 14 years old.' He pointed towards Chrissy and Michael James, 'see, the two of them didn't just hurt your daughter, Bo, my Mirela, no, long before that, they had hurt Daisy too, in the most fucking horrific way you can imagine.
 They fucking brutalized her, and her just a child, but they were pissed or drugged or both, and they found her just reading a fucking book one evening, down by the stream just on the edge of the site, and they pinned her down and raped her.'

Bo looked at his nephew and friend in disgust and knew instantly that this was the truth, and that they were monsters. The jail he'd just been freed from had been filled with men like them, and they'd been beaten and tortured in there for their crimes. He felt sick to the stomach as Patrick continued.

'She never told a soul about it up until she met me, but as we started to get close, and I told her about how they'd treated Mirela, she opened up to me. I wanted to kill the fuckers there and then, but she made me swear not to. She didn't want her mother and father to ever find out how she'd been soiled by those dirty bastards. It was only a couple of years later, when I knew it was coming time for you to be getting out, and I needed my revenge, that I came up with the plan.'

Patrick turned to look at Chrissy then, 'go on then, you fucker,' he snarled, 'I'll let you tell him how that happened.'

Bo was still trying hard to work out how this had all ended up with the two gloits opposite him, holding the only weapons he could see. But as soon as Chrissy started talking, he knew, and even though his respect for Patrick soared at the simplicity, he also knew there was no way he was going to come out of this alive.

'He fucking filmed us on a camcorder, uncle,' Chrissy said, his head still hanging,

'talked that Daisy girl into flirting with us, even though she was married to him, and she brought it all up. That night. She said she wanted to forgive us and move on with her life, but first she needed to know why we'd both raped her when she was just a child.'

He nodded towards Michael James then and continued,

'it was him who got me talking,' he said, 'I was telling her to fuck off, but he admitted it straight away, started laughing and asked her did she still like it doggy style. I just got carried away then, and we were both taking the piss, but he got it all on tape, the whole fucking confession.'

'See, Daisy loves me, Bo,' Patrick said after Chrissy had gone silent, 'almost as much as Mirela did, and she was prepared to do anything for me. That's why I ended up marrying her, she was the only one I could trust to help me get my revenge you see. I never loved her like I did Mirela, I'll never love anyone like that, but I love her well enough, and we're a family, me, her and the little man, we don't hurt each other and we stick together, something you know nothing about.'

Bo was speechless. It all made sense now. The reason Patrick himself wasn't holding a weapon was that he had no intention of getting his own hands dirty. He didn't need to, he had these two fuckers to do it for him and they couldn't refuse. Patrick had also informed him that the video footage still existed and was hidden away, guarded by Mick Keenan.

That's why Chrissy and Michael couldn't turn their weapons on Patti and get rid of the threat. He'd been wrong, so very wrong. This lad wasn't just a planner, like himself, he was fucking meticulous! His whole adult life had been completely designed on getting to this day. He shook his head in wonder and gave a little smile.

'I have to give it to you, lad,' he said, quietly, 'that's some fucking determination you have.' He shook his head and then looked Patrick straight in the eyes, 'if things had been different, me and you, we would have been unstoppable. No one could have touched us. As much as you must hate the knowledge, Patrick, you're just like me.'

'I'm fuck all like you,' Patrick said, quietly now, as though the story he'd just told had taken everything out of him, 'now, face your fate like a man and then I can finally start to fucking live in peace.'

Bo nodded, sure that he saw a tear on Patrick's face, and then turned back to Chrissy and Michael James, 'so, lads, which of you is to do the deed then? I mean if I have a choice,' he nodded at Chrissy, 'I'd sooner take a shot to the head rather than take a hiding with the crow bar from that soft bastard.'

'We have no choice,' Chrissy said, flatly, 'for years he's had that fucking tape, threatening to go to the gavvers, we'd have been locked up for longer than you for fuck's sake. And you know more than most, Bo, what they'd have done to us in there, we'd have been fucked up, and for the whole of our sentence. You must see we've no choice.'

Bo Lee thought of Mirela then, and his old ma, as he suddenly lunged forwards, trying to run, 'come on then, you cunts!' He screamed just before the shot rang out.

The end

Epilogue

Chrissy Lee and Michael James had known their fate for years. Their choice had been to go to jail for the rape of a minor, there and then, as soon as Patrick King had presented them with the evidence, or for the shooting of their uncle, a known child killer, a few years down the line. They chose the easier option. Everyone knew what happened to kiddy fiddlers in jail, and although Daisy Wright had been 14, and had never grassed on them when it had happened, it wouldn't matter. They had not only admitted it on camera, but they'd laughed about it and tormented the girl. They'd be forever known as nonces, and they knew Patrick would have turned them in, he had all the explicit evidence any judge would need.

Nobody claimed Bo Lee's body, not his brother nor any of his many cousins. He had a pauper's grave in a cemetery in Leeds where his remains had been found. He had been identified and an announcement had been made in the papers, but nobody was interested. As far as everyone was concerned, he'd got his just desserts. There had been no mourners, just a priest and two nuns had attended the funeral. A single shot to his head had removed half his face, and he'd been left in the woods to rot. It hadn't taken the police long to track down the killers. The idiots had been driving around in the same van they'd picked him up from jail in.

Violet Lee, Maureen King and Daisy Wright had all held hands as they gathered together in Bina's van on the night that Patrick had come home and announced, 'it's over', and Bina blessed them all,

'Numaj dileno ćiriklo xindel po kujbo (men are like fish – the great ones devour the small) ' she chanted, 'kushti bok.'

Printed in Great Britain
by Amazon